The Case of the

Lovable Labs

A Thousand Islands Doggy Inn Mystery

B.R. Snow

Copyright © 2017 B.R. Snow

ISBN: 978-1-942691-36-5

Website: www.brsnow.net/

Twitter:@BernSnow

Facebook: facebook.com/bernsnow

Cover Design: Reggie Cullen

Cover Photo: James R. Miller

Other Books by B.R. Snow

The Thousand Islands Doggy Inn Mysteries

- The Case of the Abandoned Aussie
- The Case of the Brokenhearted Bulldog
- The Case of the Caged Cockers
- The Case of the Dapper Dandie Dinmont
- The Case of the Eccentric Elkhound
- The Case of the Faithful Frenchie
- The Case of the Graceful Goldens
- The Case of the Hurricane Hounds
- The Case of the Itinerant Ibizan
- The Case of the Jaded Jack Russell
- The Case of the Klutzy King Charles

The Whiskey Run Chronicles

- Episode 1 – The Dry Season Approaches
- Episode 2 – Friends and Enemies
- Episode 3 – Let the Games Begin
- Episode 4 – Enter the Revenuer
- Episode 5 – A Changing Landscape
- Episode 6 – Entrepreneurial Spirits
- Episode 7 – All Hands On Deck
- The Whiskey Run Chronicles – The Complete Volume 1

The Damaged Posse

- American Midnight
- Larrikin Gene
- Sneaker World
- Summerman
- The Duplicates

Other Books

- Divorce Hotel
- Either Ore

To all the animal rescue centers in Texas and Florida

Amazing work performed by amazing people

Chapter 1

"We should have just eloped."

From the comfort of my seat at the bar, I glanced up at Sammy and felt genuine sympathy for him. Obviously exhausted, he sat down next to me and rubbed his forehead as he stared at the bottles that were backlit and gleaming on three levels of glass shelves that stretched the length of the bar. I patted his hand and waved to Millie, our new head bartender, who approached and gave Sammy a small, sad smile. I motioned for her to pour Sammy a glass of the wine I was drinking.

"I can't take it," he said, shaking his head. "My best man is hitting on every woman with a pulse, our families hate each other, Jill's sister is totally out of control, and you need a scorecard to keep track of who's dating who."

"Yeah, that part was giving me a headache," I said, taking a sip of wine. "The dating tree thing."

"I had to get out of there for a while," Sammy said, glancing back into the dining room.

"Hang in there," I said. "In a couple of days this will all be over, and you'll be honeymooning in the Caribbean."

I snuck a peek into the dining room where the tables had been arranged in a long rectangle and set for fifty. What had started out as a small rehearsal dinner had morphed into a massive celebration for family and friends. As soon as Sammy and Jill had made the decision to expand the guest list *just a bit*, the floodgates had opened, and rather than run the risk of hurting anyone's feelings, they'd decided to cast the invitation net wide. And instead of trying to juggle regular dinner guests along with the large group, we'd finally decided to close the restaurant to the general public for the evening. Now, the dining room housed a diverse collection of people connected in some way to the bride and groom; our two favorite and most valuable staff members at the Doggy Inn.

"Uh-oh," I said, laughing. "Grumpy bride alert."

Sammy turned and noticed Jill heading straight for him. She wasn't happy, but I wasn't sure if Sammy was the target of her anger. Apparently, he wasn't either and not taking any chances.

"Hey, Sweetie," he cooed, pulling the barstool next to him back.

"Yeah, whatever," she said, not sitting down. "We should have just eloped."

"Tell me about it," Sammy said. "What am I missing?"

"My mother is regaling everyone with my life story," Jill said, shaking her head. "When I got up from the table, I'd just turned ten and was getting ready to head off to summer camp."

"Brutal," I said, frowning. "Can we get you a drink?"

"No, thanks," Jill said. "We need to get back in there. As soon as my mother wraps up, they're going to serve dessert and start the toasts."

I nodded, drained my wine, and shrugged at Millie. She grinned and gave us a finger-wave as we headed back into the dining room. I sat down next to Josie who was tight-lipped and toying with her wine glass.

"What happened? Did they catch you at the border?" she whispered.

"What?"

"Your escape. Foiled, right?"

"I never made it past the bar," I said, laughing. "What did I miss?"

"Just Mr. Hands sitting next to me," she whispered. "He seems to think my thigh is some sort of armrest."

"He's lucky he didn't try that while you were eating," I said.

"You got that right," she said.

"Who is he again?" I said, frowning as I tried to remember.

"Don't you ever pay attention? He's the best man," she said, shaking her head. "And if he's the best that's out there, we're both in a lot of trouble."

"I'm sure it's just an honorary title," I said.

"Where were you, darling?"

I turned to my mother who was sitting on my left.

"I had to go over a few things with Millie in the bar," I said, lying through my teeth.

"Of course, you did," she said, raising an eyebrow at me. "And you didn't have the decency to take me with you?"

"It can't be that bad," I said, glancing around the table and trying to remember what I'd been told during introductions. "But you better catch me up."

"Well, let's see," my mother said, nodding at Jill's mother who was sitting directly across from us, but at least fifteen feet away. "The mother is currently dating the hammered guy sitting on her right."

"Who's he?"

"He's the ex-best friend of her and her ex-husband," my mother said, a small smile etched on her face.

It was the smile she brought out for town council meetings and other occasions whenever her patience was being tested or when she'd rather be anywhere else. And sometimes, like right now, both.

"The ex-husband being Jill's dad," I said, glancing down the table at him.

"Of course," she said, nodding as she sipped her wine.

"Then why didn't you just say Jill's dad?"

"I'm trying to keep the poor girl's name out of it," my mother said with a small shrug. "I can't believe those two produced such a wonderful young woman."

"Yeah, people often say the same thing about you and me," I deadpanned.

"Funny, darling." She surreptitiously pointed at the man sitting next to Jill's mother. "He was the best man at their wedding."

"This just keeps better and better."

"Apparently, they started dating right after Jill's parents split up."

"Or maybe before?"

"Nothing gets past you, darling," she said, patting my hand. "But he's been hitting on the woman to his right, one of Sammy's cousins I think, but Jill's mother has been making goo-goo eyes with the guy sitting next to Josie for the past half-hour and hasn't noticed."

"The best man? He's had his hands all over Josie," I whispered.

"I'm sure Josie can handle him," my mother said, then leaned in close and whispered. "Apparently, the mother's boyfriend has also got a little thing going with Jill's sister."

"Really?" I said, surprised. "The Princess of Darkness?"

"What?"

"That's what Chef Claire and I call her. Josie prefers Beelzebub, so take your pick."

"Yes, she does seem to be a particularly annoying woman. Josie told me that she's taking her maid of honor responsibilities very seriously," my mother said, laughing.

"She's out of her mind," I said, sneaking a glance down the table at Jill's sister who was flirting with Freddie, our good friend, and the local medical examiner. "Is the mother's boyfriend married?"

"Divorced," my mother said, taking a sip of wine. "And, obviously, quite the player."

"Thanks for the warning. Is his ex-wife here?"

"No, but she's supposed to arrive tomorrow," my mother said, frowning. "She's Jill's godmother. At least, I think that's right. I'm going to need a scorecard to keep it all straight."

"This must be driving Jill's dad nuts," I said. "His ex-wife and daughter are both sleeping with the guy who used to be his best friend?"

"And also sleeping with his sister," my mother said, raising an eyebrow at me and nodding at a woman who was chatting with Jackson, another good friend of ours.

"Wow," I said, shaking my head. "I guess the guy likes to keep it in the family. I'm surprised Jill even decided to invite him. This could get ugly."

"I don't think she did," my mother said. "He's here as her mother's plus-one."

I glanced down the table where Jill's father was sitting next to her. He was whispering earnestly in her ear, and she tolerated the one-sided conversation with a blank stare and the occasional nod.

"I'm sorry," I said, glancing across the table and focusing on the man sitting next to Jill's mother. "I couldn't hear what you said."

"I said you two must be sisters," he said, grinning back and forth at my mother and me.

"Geez, how old do you think I am?" I deadpanned across the table.

"Oh, no…that isn't what I was-"

"Funny, darling," my mother snapped, then smiled at him. "You're too kind, sir."

"Oh, please," he said, playfully waving my mother's formality away. "Call me, Roger."

"Roger it is," my mother said, then refocused on me. "Have you met Jill's sister yet?"

"Just over the phone. We've had mandatory conference calls twice a week for the past month," I said, shaking my head. "She's a real piece of work."

"She seems to have taken a shine to Freddie," my mother said. "She's cute. As far as out of control maids of honor go."

"We have a meeting with her and Jill tomorrow. Apparently, she wants to make a few last-minute changes."

"Changes to what?"

"I have no idea."

"Geez, please tell me you didn't do that," Josie said, staring down.

"I'm so sorry," the man sitting next to her said, grabbing a napkin and reaching for her lap. "I'm such a klutz."

"Thanks," Josie said, grabbing his hand and stopping it in its tracks. "I think I've got it from here."

"That's a lot of wine," I said, staring down at the massive red stain on her gray slacks. "C'mon, let's see what we can do about that."

"A rather clever ruse to get away, dear," my mother whispered with a grin.

"You just wish you'd thought of it, Mom," I said, standing up. "We'll be right back."

Josie wiped up what she could with her napkin, then tossed it on the table. She followed me toward the ladies' room. We walked in, and Josie removed her slacks and placed them on the counter next to the sink.

"Remember to blot, don't rub," she said, reaching for the dispenser that contained the paper towels. "What a mess. I just bought these. I'll never get it all out."

"Relax," I said, waiting for her to hand me some of the towels. "We just need to get working on it before it dries."

"Perfect," she said, shaking her head. "We're out of paper towels."

"Hang on."

I headed for the large cedar closet that ran along the back wall of the bathroom. I grabbed my keys from my pocket and unlocked the closet. I stepped inside and searched for paper towels. Moments later, I exited and closed the door and shook my head.

"There's none in here. How can we possibly be out of paper towels?"

"Check next door in the men's room."

"The men's room?" I said, frowning. "Geez, I don't know about that."

"Don't be such a baby. Just knock first, and then go in," Josie said, shaking her head. "C'mon, hurry up. You're wasting time."

"All right. Hold your horses," I said, heading for the door.

I knocked on the men's room door, heard nothing, then poked my head inside. It was empty, and I headed straight for the cedar closet identical to the one in the women's bathroom. I unlocked it and stepped inside. I grabbed three packets of paper towels then heard the bathroom door open. Before I could make my presence known, the unseen man, whistling to himself, approached one of the urinals. I decided to wait it out and pulled the door closed. I did my best to ignore what was happening only a few feet away from where I was standing. Eventually, I heard the sound of flushing, then the sound of running water. The man turned the water off, continued to whistle as he removed some paper towels from the dispenser to dry his hands. I heard the door open and was just about to leave the closet when I heard him speak. I recognized Roger's voice immediately and frowned.

"Wow, look who's here," he said. "I'm shocked. But what a nice surprise."

I listened closely, but the man's visitor was whispering, and I couldn't make out a word she was saying. I worked my head up and down and tried to see through the cedar slats in the door, but they were angled down, and I could only catch the occasional glimpse of their feet.

"Whoa," Roger said, laughing. "Really? Here?"

I pressed my ear against the door, but I could only hear the faint sound of the woman's whisper.

"An hour?" Roger said. "Oh, don't worry. I'll be there."

Then I heard a soft rattle that sounded familiar, but I couldn't place it.

"Of course," Roger said, laughing. "Fresh breath before kissing. How could I forget?"

I nodded when the rattle finally registered. I pondered the incongruity of the unseen woman's need to have minty-fresh breath before allowing herself to make out in a germ-infested public restroom. I came up a little short on that one.

"Whoa," Roger said. "Getting right to it, huh? You and your magic tongue." Then he softly gagged and coughed. "You are in the mood, aren't you? You shoved that mint right down my throat."

"Yuk," I whispered with a grimace.

"Wow, what a great kiss. As always," Roger said, exhaling audibly. "Okay, I should get back. But I'll be seeing you in an hour."

Then I heard the door open and another short burst of running water. I stood quietly leaning against the closet door, then heard the bathroom door open and close a second time. I waited a few seconds then slowly stepped out of the closet and glanced around. Then I made a beeline for the exit and headed back to the ladies' room where Josie was leaning with her back against the sink and her arms folded across her chest. She glared at me and grabbed one of the packets of paper towels from my hands.

"What on earth took you so long?" she said, blotting a handful of the paper towels on her slacks.

"I got trapped in there," I said as I began working on another section of the stain. "Roger walked in while I was in the supply closet."

"And you decided to stay?" she said, raising an eyebrow at me.

"He had company."

"Really? Female company?"

"Yeah."

"In the bathroom? Yuk," she said, frowning.

"They were only making out," I said. "But they made plans to meet up in an hour."

"Who was the woman?"

"I couldn't tell. I had the closet door closed, and she was whispering the whole time."

"You think it was Jill's mom?"

"I guess it could have been," I said, shrugging. "But they're sitting right next to each other at the table. They wouldn't need to sneak off to have that conversation. Maybe it was the Princess of Darkness."

"He's sleeping with Beelzebub?"

"Apparently."

"Well, for his sake, I hope he takes instructions well," Josie said, grabbing a fresh handful of paper towels.

I laughed and continued to work on the wine stain.

"He's been doing the roving eye thing all night," Josie said. "Maybe he connected with one of the other women at the table."

"There must be at least a half-dozen possible candidates," I said. "I wonder who it is."

Josie shrugged as she tossed the used paper towels in the trash and pulled her slacks back on. She left her blouse untucked and managed to cover the top half of the wine stain.

"Well, that's the best I can do," she said, looking at herself in the mirror. "Let's go get some dessert."

I followed her out the door and back to the table. We sat down, and I glanced across the table at Roger who was back in his seat and chatting with Jill's mother. She was laughing at something he said, and I followed his eyes to see if he might reveal the identity of the person he was meeting later. But apart from a casual glance at his watch, he didn't give anything away.

The servers arrived with dessert trays displaying a variety of selections. We waited patiently for one of the trays to make it to our end of the table then helped ourselves. We sipped coffee and ate our dessert in relative silence. By the time I finished, I was officially full and ready to head home to play with the dogs. But before we could say our goodbyes, Roger tapped a wine glass with a spoon, and silence followed. He got to his feet, paused for effect, then looked around the table.

"I'd like to make a toast," he said. "But before I do, I suppose I should grab my glass of champagne. That might help, huh?" He chuckled as he continued to search for his glass. "What the heck did I do with it?"

"Here, have this one," Jill's mother said, handing him a full glass that was sitting near her.

"Perfect," he said, giving her a slight bow. He picked the glass up, took a sip, then held it out toward Sammy and Jill who were sitting at the other end of the table. "I can't tell you what an honor it is to be here with all of you tonight."

Jill's father, still sitting next to her, snorted audibly, then his face turned red with embarrassment. He sat back in his chair and gestured for Roger to get on with it.

"Thanks for your input, Bill," Roger said, frowning at the interruption. "Eloquent as always." He took another sip of champagne and focused on Sammy and Jill. "I want to wish the happy couple the absolute best for a lifetime of love and joy. To Sammy and Jill."

"To Sammy and Jill," the rest of the table repeated as they raised their glasses.

Roger raised the glass to his lips, was about to drink, then dropped his glass, blinked several times, and clutched his stomach. The glass shattered on the floor, and Roger fell face first into his chocolate mousse. Everyone around the table stared at him, then frowned at their own glasses and set them down.

"Okay," Josie said, gently setting her glass down. "I think we might have some bad champagne."

"Have you been drinking it?" I said, pushing my glass away.

"Only all night," Josie said.

"Then you'll be fine," I said.

"You really think so?"

"You're not dead yet."

"But I do have a bit of a tummy ache."

"You just inhaled four different desserts," I said, glancing over at her.

"Yeah, I guess that could be it," Josie said, staring at Roger. "What do you think? Is he dead?"

"Not sure. But I don't think he's gonna make his hookup."

Chapter 2

Roger was, in fact, dead.

Freddie, in his role as the medical examiner, confirmed it soon after he jumped out of his seat to check on Roger's condition. And when he frowned and looked around the table with a sad shake of his head, most of the people at the table made a beeline for another section of the dining room or the bar. The next two hours were predictable, and a confused, hushed buzz filled the restaurant as we waited it out from the comfort of the lounge area in the bar. None of the other guests had the same reaction to the champagne, which led me to deduce that we were probably dealing with a single tainted glass of bubbly. But just to be sure, most of the guests switched to beer or wine, and the open champagne bottles were capped and set aside for lab testing.

Chief Abrams, our chief of police, and two detectives from the state police interviewed all the guests, then sent them on their way with instructions not to leave town. Since everyone would be attending the wedding in two days, I doubted the Chief's mandate was necessary. But he was a by-the-book kind of guy who didn't like leaving any loose ends. He and Freddie entered the lounge, spotted us sitting on a couch and plopped down in nearby chairs. The Chief slid his notebook into the inside pocket of his suit jacket.

"I feel bad for those two," he said, nodding at Sammy and Jill who were sitting by themselves in a back corner of the lounge, still in a state of shock. "Great way to start the pre-wedding events, huh?"

"Yeah, I'm sure it wasn't what they had planned," I said, my neurons idling, but ready to get rolling. "What did you come up with?"

"Well, we certainly have a long list of suspects," he said, shaking his head. "Seven women either confirmed they'd dated the guy in the past or were currently thinking about it."

"Were any of them eating breath mints while you were talking to them?" I said.

"You could have given me a million tries, and I wouldn't have guessed that was the question she was going to ask," Freddie said, shaking his head.

Josie snorted.

"No, I don't think so," Chief Abrams said, giving me a confused frown. "But I can't say that I was really paying attention to that particular detail. Talk to me, Suzy."

I recounted my story about the earlier events in the men's room. The Chief and Freddie both listened closely.

"Can I ask you what you were doing in the men's room?" the Chief said.

"I went in there looking for paper towels and got trapped in the closet," I said, shrugging.

"And the woman made him eat a breath mint before she would kiss him?" the Chief said.

"That's what it sounded like based on what he was saying," I said. "I never really heard her voice. She was whispering the whole time."

"Okay, that might be something worth checking out," the Chief said.

"You think somebody slipped some sort of poison into his glass of champagne, right?"

"Nothing gets past you," Josie said, laughing.

"Don't start," I said.

"That's certainly our working theory at the moment," Chief Abrams said. "But from where I was sitting, it looked like Jill's mother handed the victim her glass."

"I don't think it was her glass," I said, frowning. "But it was definitely sitting right next to her."

"Maybe the poison was intended for her," Josie said.

"That thought definitely crossed my mind," the Chief said. "I just wish the glass hadn't shattered when he dropped it. It's going to make it a lot harder to analyze."

"Who'd want to kill Jill's mom?" Josie said.

"Maybe her ex-husband," the Chief said, shrugging. "Or maybe one of the other women felt neglected by Roger and decided to take her out."

"Nah, I don't like it," I said. "I think Roger was definitely the target."

"But how could the killer be sure he'd end up with that glass of champagne?" Chief Abrams said.

"That's a really good question," I said.

"Thanks. That's why they pay me the big bucks," he said, then turned to Freddie. "How long before you get the toxicology report back?"

"If we put a rush on it, and are really nice to the folks in the lab, at best, maybe a couple of days," Freddie said.

"The results won't be back before the wedding?" I said.

"I doubt it," Freddie said.

"Why does it take so long? It can't be that hard to figure it out." I said.

"It's not," Freddie said. "You just slice him open and start digging around."

"Okay, that's enough, Freddie," Josie said, frowning.

"Hey, she asked. But the lab has a hard time keeping up with demand. I guess you could say it's a growth industry," he said, laughing at his own joke. "Are you sure they're even going ahead with the wedding?"

"Geez, I hadn't even considered that," I said. "But they have guests here from all over the place. They have to go through with it, right?"

"Would you?" Josie said.

I thought about it.

"I'm not sure if I would," I said, shrugging. "The guy was a close friend of the family, at least he was once, but he wasn't related. And based on the looks Jill's dad was giving him all night, I doubt if he'd let them cancel the wedding over him."

"Tough call," Chief Abrams said. "That was a fast-acting poison. He took two sips before he finished the toast, then he hit the deck." He looked at Freddie. "What does that tell you?"

"That the guy couldn't hold his booze?" Freddie deadpanned, then frowned when his joke was met with silence. "My initial guess would be cyanide. It doesn't take long to do its thing once it's ingested. But we'll know soon enough."

"Is the body still in the dining room?" I said, glancing over my shoulder.

"No, he was bagged and tagged then wheeled out the back of the restaurant a few minutes ago. They'll start panning for gold soon."

"Really, Freddie," I said, frowning. "Must you?"

"Hey, you asked. Why do you want to know?"

"Since he was in the bathroom with a woman just before he died, I'm just wondering if she might have left traces of something on the body. You know, like a lipstick smear, the smell of perfume. They were definitely snuggling."

"If there is, they'll find it," Freddie said, grabbing his phone from his pocket. "But that's a good thought." He placed a call, had a quick word with someone, then put his phone away. "Slight lipstick smudge on the inside of his right collar."

"Is that useful?" Josie said.

"It could be," Freddie said, nodding. "The science is amazing these days. Not only will they be able to do some work on the DNA, but there's also a chance they'll be able to identify the actual brand of lipstick."

"Really?" Josie said. "How is that possible?"

"Like I said, the science is incredible. Basically, there are three techniques that involve the use of chromatography," Freddie said, effortlessly slipping into a technical description. "High-performance chromatography, gas chromatography, thin-layer chromatographic."

"I'm sensing a theme," Josie said, laughing.

"Generally, a sample is injected into a machine to be analyzed, and the results are fed into a computer. I can go a lot deeper into the technical process if you like."

"Uh, no, thanks," Josie said, flashing him a small smile.

"Good call," he said. "It even bores me. But unlike your favorite cop shows, that testing is going to take a lot longer than your basic toxicology report."

"How long?" I said.

"My guess is at least a week," he said. "Possibly longer. It's complicated and very specialized work. And we're usually at the mercy of the lab's workload."

"I doubt if the killer was the woman who was snogging with Roger in the bathroom," Josie said.

"Yeah, I agree. That doesn't make much sense," I said. "From what I could tell, she was rather fond of him."

"My money is on Beelzebub," Josie said. "I don't like her."

"Who?" Freddie said, frowning.

"Your new girlfriend," I said. "We couldn't help notice that you two were getting pretty cozy at dinner."

"Faith?" Freddie said. "What's wrong with her? She's cute as all get out. And very friendly."

"Knock yourself out," Josie said.

"Why on earth would you suspect her?" Freddie said.

"Because she had something going on with the victim," I said.

"What?" Freddie stared at me in disbelief, then glanced at Chief Abrams. The Chief confirmed the news with a nod of his head. "But he's gotta be at least twenty, maybe thirty, years older than she is."

"She put it right out there as soon as I asked her how well she knew the victim," the Chief said. "It almost sounded like she was proud of it."

"Was she distraught?" I said to the Chief.

"No, that's not the word I'd use. She was definitely upset, but I think she was more concerned about the impact it might have on the wedding."

"That sounds about right," Josie said.

"Well, I like her. And not that it's any of your business, but we're going out later tonight," Freddie said. "She said she's always wanted to take a boat ride at night."

"You're going out on the River tonight?" I said.

"Yeah, we are," Freddie said. "A nice ride in the moonlight."

"Bring some champagne. Maybe we'll get lucky," Josie deadpanned.

"Harsh," I said.

"Yeah, maybe a little."

"Oh, there you are. I've been looking all over for you," the Princess of Darkness aka Beelzebub said as she approached.

"Hi, Faith," Freddie said, sitting upright in his seat. "Are you ready to go?"

"Almost," she said, barely looking at him before focusing on Josie and me. "You're Suzy and Josie, right?"

"In the flesh," Josie said.

"I'm sorry we didn't get a chance to chat during dinner. It's so nice to finally meet you. But after all those phone calls, it's like we're old friends, right?"

"Sure, sure."

"Don't forget, we're meeting tomorrow morning at your office. Nine o'clock sharp," Faith said.

"Oh, we'll be there," Josie said with a coy smile. "Before I forget, are you a dog lover?"

"No, not at all," she said, shaking her head. "I hate dogs."

"I knew it," Josie whispered.

"What?"

"Nothing.

"Actually, I'm scared to death of dogs. Why do you ask?"

"It's just that we run a dog business," Josie said. "And I want to make sure we're prepared for your visit."

I glanced down at the floor to hide my grin.

"Yes, I'm well aware of what you do for a living," Faith said, glancing around. "But they're all in cages, right?"

"Well, technically we like to consider them condos," Josie said.

"They all have their own condo?" Faith said, frowning.

"Sure," Josie deadpanned. "One bedroom, one bath, cable and wireless ready, view of the River."

"Got it," Faith said, glaring at Josie. "I don't need anybody else trying to make me feel stupid. I already have my family for that."

"She was just joking, Faith," I said, laughing. "We'll see you in the morning."

"Nine o'clock sharp," she said, reaching into her pocket. "We have a lot to cover." She removed a plastic container and shook it. "Mint?" She popped a small handful into her mouth and offered them to everyone. Freddie was the only one who accepted.

"Okay, you kids have fun," Josie said.

"I don't like my chances, but maybe I'll be pleasantly surprised," Faith said, nodding her head at Freddie to get to his feet. Then she pointed at the door, and Freddie managed a small wave as he headed for the exit. She cleared her throat as he was about to open the door, and he pulled the door open and took a step back to give her plenty of room to walk past him. "Nine o'clock sharp," she said, without looking back.

"Well, that was pleasant," Josie said. "You know what I like best about her?"

"Nothing?"

"Exactly."

"She certainly didn't seem very distraught."

"Yeah, I noticed," Josie said.

"What do you think, Chief?" I said.

"Indifferent to the fact the guy she was sleeping with is dead and completely self-absorbed," the Chief said, frowning. "Pretty consistent with how she seemed when I interviewed her earlier."

"Not to mention she was popping breath mints by the handful," I said.

"Yeah, I think we'll put her on the list," the Chief said.

"We'll see what we can come up with tomorrow morning," I said.

"If she lives long enough to tell her side of the story."

"Do you need any help?" I said to her.

"Help with what?"

"Deciding how to incorporate the dogs into the meeting," I said, grinning at her.

"No, thanks. I've got that one covered," she said, beaming back at me.

Chapter 3

I tapped the keyboard, stared at the monitor, then glanced up at Josie who was peering over my shoulder. She shrugged, and we both refocused on the screen image that hadn't changed since we'd sat down ten minutes ago.

"It's been a while since I've tried to use the registration system," I said. "Think we should give Sammy and Jill a call?"

"They're officially on vacation," Josie said. "And I'm sure they have other things on their mind today."

"You mean, like the dead guy in the restaurant?" I said, tapping the keyboard to no avail.

"Nothing gets past you."

The front door opened and Sammy stepped inside. He saw us hovering around the computer and headed straight for us.

"What are you doing here?" Josie said.

"I forgot my phone yesterday," he said, opening a drawer next to the computer and retrieving it. "Let me guess. You can't get into the system."

"I think it's broken," I said, staring forlornly at the screen.

"Did you read the notes we left you?" he said, pointing at the piece of paper that was taped to the bottom corner of the screen.

"Uh, no," I said, feeling my face redden.

"Way to go, Suzy," Josie said, gently punching my shoulder.

"I noticed you didn't see it either."

"I was too busy trying to supervise you," she said, grinning at Sammy.

I read from the paper.

"Item one, enter password to end system timeout." I frowned at Sammy. "System timeout? The computer takes timeouts?"

"Yeah, it gets three per half," Sammy said with a sad shake of his head.

"Funny."

"How can you be so good searching the web but so bad with the basics?" he said.

"I'm fine once I get in," I said, then looked down at the page of notes. I typed the password that was printed in block letters then pressed the enter key. The image on the screen dissolved, and the landing page of the registration system appeared. "Hah. Got it. Thanks, Sammy."

"Just read the notes, okay? Look, Jill and Faith are on their way over, so I'm getting out of here," Sammy said. "I can only take her in very short doses."

"That's probably something you should have considered before you asked her to marry you," Josie deadpanned.

"Not funny," Sammy said, making a face at Josie. "You'd think Faith was the one who was getting married. She is incredibly annoying."

"No argument there," Josie said. "Did you guys talk about the wedding last night?"

"We were up most of the night talking about it," Sammy said. "But we finally decided not to cancel it."

"Good for you," I said. "How's Jill holding up?"

"She's still a little shaky. And really mad at her mom for bringing the guy with her to the wedding. You know, it's like she's rubbing it in her dad's face. Then her mom decided that we should do some sort of tribute to Roger. That set off another hour of arguments. So, we're going to work in a short memorial service before the ceremony," he said. "Does that sound weird?"

"Maybe a little," Josie said. "But it should be interesting. I don't think I've ever been to a wedding that had a warm-up act."

"Don't start," I said, fighting back a chuckle.

"I guess we could have postponed it," Sammy said, running his hands through his hair. "But we finally decided we couldn't face the prospect of going through all this a second time."

Josie and I both nodded. I patted his hand and smiled at him.

"You did good. And it's going to be fine."

"I hope so," he said. "Okay, I'm getting out of here before they show up. Oh, and I almost forgot to mention it. Jill's godmother is going to stop by and drop off her dogs as soon as she gets into town."

"Her godmother?" I said, pausing to connect the dots. "Roger's ex-wife, right?"

"Yeah. That's going to make things even weirder," Sammy said.

"How did she take the news?" Josie said.

"She had her phone turned off last night. We left her a ton of messages, but we're still not sure if she's heard the news yet."

"Did you say dogs, as in plural?" I said, studying the screen.

"Yeah, she has three," Sammy said. "She didn't say what kind. All she told Jill over the phone was that she has three little dogs that needed to be boarded for a couple of days. I reserved one of the big condos. It's under McNamara."

"Got it," I said, studying the screen. "It says to expect her to get here around ten. Where is she coming in from?"

"She lives somewhere in New Hampshire," Sammy said. "It's a long drive, and I imagine she broke it up into two days. I'm not sure where she spent the night. But she refused to put the dogs on a plane and couldn't bear to leave them behind."

"Good for her," I said, nodding. "She sounds like our kind of people."

"Jill loves her and says she great," Sammy said. "But Faith can't stand her. And from what I hear, the feeling is mutual."

"Then I know I'm going to like her," Josie said. "Okay, get out of here and go enjoy your last day of freedom."

"That's right," I said with a grin. "How are you spending the day?"

"I'm going to take the boat out. Tripod and I are going to relax and cruise the River."

Tripod was Sammy's three-legged cocker spaniel that had lost a leg to frostbite. Josie had performed the surgery, and we had nursed him back to health at the Inn before Sammy decided to adopt him. Now, Tripod was a regular visitor, and Sammy often brought him to work.

Sammy glanced out the window, then turned back to us.

"Okay, there they are. And I'm out of here," he said, heading for the front door. "I'll see you tomorrow at the church."

He held the door open for both women, gave Jill a hug and a kiss then departed with a wave. Soon, we heard the sound of his car pulling out of the driveway. Jill entered with a sad smile and a small wave. Josie and I both gave her a long hug. Faith casually strolled to the center of the reception area and stood there twirling her sunglasses.

"And this is where I work," Jill said.

"So I surmised," Faith said, glancing around the room with a grimace. "What's that smell?"

"Eau de Dog," Josie said.

"You really should do something about that," she said, sniffing. "It's rather unpleasant."

I placed a hand on Josie's shoulder to calm her down. Jill also noticed the tension in the room.

"Why don't we get started?" Jill said. "The sooner we do, the quicker we'll finish."

"Are you sure you're up for this?" I said.

"Yeah, I'm fine," Jill said.

"Roger's gone, and there's nothing we can do about it," Faith said, still glancing around her surroundings and obviously not liking what she was seeing.

"How's your mom doing?" I said, ignoring the Princess of Darkness.

"Apparently, the police grilled her pretty hard, but they turned her loose just after midnight," Jill said.

"I imagine they had a lot of questions for her since she was sitting next to him."

"Not to mention the fact that she was the one who handed him the glass of champagne," Jill said, shaking her head. "And when she finally got home, she felt it was necessary to tell us the whole story of what she's calling her *unwarranted incarceration*. By the time we finished, it was almost four. She's still sleeping."

"Are you really sure you want to go ahead with the wedding?" I said.

"Of course, we're going ahead with the wedding," Faith said, her voice rising a notch. "I think we've had just about enough of the *let's just cancel the wedding* conversations."

"Wow," Josie whispered.

"Do you have something to say?" Faith said, wheeling around to face Josie.

"Oh, I've got a lot to say," Josie said, giving her a death stare.

"Let's not, shall we?" I said, gesturing for everyone to sit down. We got settled into our seats, and I focused on Faith. "So, how was your date with Freddie last night?"

"The undertaker? I guess it was okay," she said with a shrug. "I should have brought a sweater. I froze my butt off."

"Medical examiner," Josie said.

"What?"

"Freddie's a medical examiner, not an undertaker," Josie said.

"What's the difference?" Faith said.

"About six feet of dirt. I'd be happy to demonstrate."

"Isn't this nice?" I said, shaking my head at Jill. "So, what do we need to talk about? I thought we had everything pretty much ready to go."

Jill nodded at her sister. Faith replaced the glare she was giving Josie with a canned smile and glanced down at the folder she had in her hand. She opened it and scanned the first page.

"First, we need to talk about your shoes," Faith said.

"What about our shoes?" I said, frowning at her.

"They're the wrong size heel," she said. "We're going to be uneven in the photos. The maid of honor and the bridesmaids should all be the same height."

"Says who?" Josie said.

"Says me. The maid of honor."

"What size heel were you thinking?" I said, placing a hand on Josie's forearm.

"Well, both of you are pretty short. And in my heels, I'm going to be just over five-foot-ten."

"Then wear smaller heels," Josie said, shrugging.

"Oh, that's too funny," Faith said, giving her a crocodile smile. "No, I'm afraid that just won't work. My dress has already been calibrated to match the size of my heels."

"Calibrated?" Josie said, glancing over at me.

"Let it go."

"You'll just need to find some bigger heels," Faith said. "If you don't, I'm going to end up looking like someone on stilts standing next to both of you."

"If you think I'm going to traipse around in six-inch heels all day, you're out of your mind," Josie said.

"Are you going to fight me on this?" Faith said, giving Josie a cold stare.

"I thought you'd never ask," Josie said, getting to her feet. "What's it gonna be, pistols or a good old-fashioned fistfight?"

"Jill, I'm going to need your help on this one," Faith said, frowning at her sister.

"Sorry, Faith. But it's their call," Jill said, then she brightened when a thought came to mind. "And since you'll be the tallest one in the bridesmaid photos, everyone's eyes will be drawn to you."

"I guess," Faith said, giving it some thought.

"That makes sense," Josie said, nodding. "But you might want to do some landscaping on those eyebrows."

"What's wrong with my eyebrows?" Faith said, gently touching them.

"Nothing that a good pair of hedge clippers wouldn't fix."

Faith glared at Josie and stood up. She took a step forward and gestured with both hands for Josie to bring it on.

"She's joking," I said, stepping between the two women. "You look fantastic. Doesn't she look great, Jill?"

"Absolutely," Jill said.

Jill and I beamed at Faith who pursed her lips, then drew a line through what I assumed was the first item on her list. We'd dodged a bullet on the shoes. I was already having enough trouble walking in my bridesmaid dress in bare feet around the house.

"Okay, next item," she said. "Pictures."

"What about them?" Jill said.

"I walked the church grounds yesterday, and I think we should move the photo session right after the ceremony to the garden in back of the church."

"I don't think you want to do that," I said.

"Oh, I most certainly do," Faith said. "The lilac is blooming, and it's going to look great as a backdrop for my...our dresses."

"It's really not a good idea, Faith," Jill said. "You should listen to Suzy on this one."

"But that lilac is spectacular."

"Yes, it is," I said, nodding. "But it's also incredibly popular with the bees. They love the stuff."

"The frontier woman is afraid of a few bees?" Faith said, laughing.

"Frontier woman?" I whispered to Josie.

"She's probably seen some of your outfits," Josie said.

"Funny," I said, then refocused on Faith. "I really need to warn you, Faith. I don't think that's a good idea."

Faith waved me off and glanced down at her list.

"Next item. I'll need to see a copy of your toasts sometime before the ceremony," she said, glancing up.

"What?" Josie said.

"A copy of the toast you're going to give the happy couple. Obviously, as the maid of honor, my toast will follow yours as the bridesmaids. And I don't want to run the risk that your speeches will pre-empt any remarks I might be making."

"I don't think that's really necessary, Faith," Jill said.

"You let me worry about that, Jill," Faith said, holding up her hand. "Relax and leave everything to me. I'm just doing everything I can to make sure your day is perfect."

"That's a very generous offer. What time are you leaving town?" Josie deadpanned.

"What?" Faith said, staring hard at Josie.

"You got anything prepared?" I said to Josie, tugging at her sleeve to get her attention.

"You're joking, right? I was just planning on winging it."

"*Winging it* is not an option," Faith said. "So, if you could get me something in the morning, that would be great." She glanced down at her list again. "Okay, now this one may be a bit contentious."

"This oughta be good," Josie whispered, shaking her head.

"Shhh."

"I took another look at our dresses," Faith said, removing a color photo from the folder. "And while I'm perfectly happy with mine, I thought that you, as the two bridesmaids, should be wearing a different dress from me."

"You want us to change our dresses? The day before the wedding?" Josie said.

"Sure. Why not?" Faith said.

"Well, for starters, because we shelled out eight hundred bucks for the ones we already have," Josie said. "And they fit perfectly."

"That won't be a problem," Faith said. "I took the liberty of dropping by the local tailor's shop yesterday. And the woman who runs the place said she would be happy to make any necessary alterations to your new dresses this afternoon. So, we should move this meeting along. We don't want to leave it to the last minute."

"Yeah, nobody wants that," I said, glancing at Jill who looked like she wanted to crawl away and hide.

"Jill," Josie said, staring at the bride to be. "You and I need to have a private chat."

"Hang on," I said, grabbing Josie's shoulder. "You *bought* new dresses for us?"

"I did," Faith said. "But don't worry, you can pay me back later. I have them out in the car. Jill, why don't you be a dear and run out and grab them?"

Jill slowly got out of her seat and made her way to the front door.

"While we're waiting, here's a picture of the dress," Faith said, handing me a photo.

"Oh, my," I said, grimacing as I stared at it. "Geez, that's a lot of orange."

"Where did you find it?" Josie said, squinting hard. "Prison Bride Quarterly?"

"I think it's lovely," Faith said.

"Then you wear it," Josie said.

"No, that's impossible," Faith said. "My outfit is locked in."

"So are ours," Josie said, giving her a death stare.

If the conversation kept going in the direction it was headed, I'd soon need a striped shirt and a whistle. I decided to try upbeat in an attempt to lighten the mood.

"Well, let's at least take a look at it first," I said. "Maybe it won't be that bad." I glanced at the door when Jill returned carrying two garment bags. She unzipped one of them and removed the dress. I stared at it then shook my head. "No, I was wrong. That's horrid."

"Good word."

"Thanks. But I'm not quite sure it tells the whole story," I said, staring at Faith. "I'm sorry, but I am not wearing that dress."

"I see," Faith said, not even trying to hide her contempt. "Then if it's not too much trouble, I'd love to hear your reasons."

"How long have you got?" Josie said, running her hands over the material.

"I think I've had about enough of this," Faith said, glancing at Jill. "We need to swing by the florist. I'd like to take another look at the table arrangements for the reception."

"Oh, I almost forgot. Hang on for a sec," Josie said, heading for the door that led into the back of the Inn. "We have something for you."

"That's right," I said, turning to Jill. "We got you a little going away present."

"You didn't need to do that."

"Don't worry. It's just a little something for you to wear in Cayman on your honeymoon."

Faith checked her watch and impatiently glanced around while we waited. A few moments later, Josie entered carrying a wrapped gift box. She handed it to Jill and gave her another hug. Then Faith noticed the trail of dogs that had followed Josie into the reception area. She gasped, let loose with a loud shriek, then jumped up and stood on top of a chair.

"You probably don't want to do that," Josie said, shaking her head.

"Oh, I'm pretty sure I do," Faith said, her eyes darting back and forth at the dogs.

"They're just going to think you want to play," Josie said.

Josie's massive Newfie, Captain, led the way across the room, and he sat down in front of Faith's chair then stood on his back legs. Despite the fact that she was standing on the chair, Captain's front paws still reached her waist. Immobilized by fear, Faith stared down at the Newfie whose tail was wagging furiously. Chloe, my Australian Shepherd, hopped up on the chair next to her and dropped the tennis ball she was carrying between the woman's feet. Then she nuzzled Faith's ankles, encouraging her to reach down and pick it up. Al and Dente, Chef Claire's Golden Retrievers, approached and sat on either side of Captain staring up at the panic-stricken woman. But it was Tiny, our Great Dane, that sent her over the edge. He nuzzled Faith's knees, then began licking her shins. Faith screamed, waved her arms, then fell backward over the chair onto the floor. All of the dogs took this as an invitation to join her on the floor for some roughhousing, and they surrounded her. She waved her arms and kicked her legs, then scrambled to her feet, and raced out the front door. The dogs, apparently puzzled by the woman's reaction, cocked their heads at us.

"Yeah, I know. Goofy, huh?" Josie said, reaching down to rub Captain's head. "What a good boy."

"She's scared of dogs?" Jill said, laughing. "I did not know that."

"Who knows, maybe it'll come in handy," I said.

"I thought it just did," Josie said. "Go ahead and open your present."

Jill smiled and removed the wrapping paper. Then she opened the box and removed a very small two-piece bathing suit.

"Really?" she said, turning it over in her hands.

"It's for those days when just the two of you are hanging out by the pool," I said.

"I have dinner napkins bigger than this," Jill said. "Do you wear something like this when you're down there?"

"Sure, sure."

Josie snorted.

"Shut it," I said, glaring at her. "But be careful you don't burn."

"Yeah," Josie said, nodding. "Put on as much sunscreen you could ever imagine you'd need, then triple it."

"Thanks," Jill said, putting the suit back in the box. Then she sighed audibly. "I should get going."

"Are you sure you're okay?" I said.

"I think so. I just never thought somebody would end up getting poisoned at my rehearsal dinner."

"Did you know that Roger and your sister had a thing going on?" I said.

"I did," Jill said, shrugging. "I never understood it. And Roger was never one of my favorite people, especially ever since I found out he was one of the major reasons my folks got divorced. But Faith has always done pretty much whatever she wanted, and it's really none of my business."

"Why do you think she was attracted to him?" I said, frowning. "He was a lot older, not to mention the fact that he was dating your mom."

"The age thing didn't bother her," Jill said. "But the fact that he was dating my mom made all the difference in the world to Faith."

"Faith saw it as some sort of competition with your mom?" Josie said.

"They have a really strange relationship," Jill said. "My mother looks at Faith and sees herself as she used to be. Faith looks at my mother as the woman she might become. And neither one of them is very happy with what they see and are scared to death. Weird, huh?"

"I guess that's a word for it," I said, then finally gave into my neurons that were insisting I ask the question. "This is probably going to sound very insensitive, but do you think it's possible that either one of them could have poisoned Roger?"

Josie punched me on the shoulder.

"Ow."

"Give it a rest, Snoopmeister," she said, shaking her head at me. "The woman is getting married tomorrow."

"No, it's okay, Josie," Jill said. "I've been asking myself that question since last night."

"See? It's a reasonable question to ask," I said, making a face at Josie. Then I focused on Jill. "What did you come up with?"

"I don't think either one of them could have done it," she said, shaking her head. "Self-absorbed is one thing, murder is something else altogether."

All three of us let the comment sink in, then Jill hugged both of us.

"I need to go make sure she's stopped screaming. Hopefully, she's cooled off by now, or it's going to be a very long day. Thanks again for everything. I'll see you guys in the morning," she said, heading toward the door. "And thanks for the swimsuit. Sammy's gonna love it."

We stood there until we heard the sound of her car driving off. Josie glanced around at the dogs and waved for them to follow her.

"Okay, guys. Great job," Josie said. "Your work is done. Who's ready for a *snack*?"

The dogs scrambled across the reception area and disappeared through the door that led to the condos. A few minutes later, Josie returned and sat down next to me behind the registration counter.

"It's been a long time since we've handled check-in," she said, putting her feet up on the counter.

"Yeah, remember when we first got started, and we had to take turns covering the front desk?"

"I do. That was a long time ago, huh?"

"Yeah. We've come a long way," I said, nodding. "Any regrets?"

"Other than the fact that Captain didn't give Beelzebub a little love bite, not a one," she said, reaching for the bag of bite-sized.

"Yeah, that would have been good," I said, grabbing a small handful.

Chapter 4

Chief Abrams stopped by the Inn about an hour after Jill and her sister had left. Trailing at his heels was his basset hound, Wally, a regular guest at the Inn whenever the Chief's wife was traveling, and he was working long hours. Josie had been the dog's vet since he was a puppy, and Wally was one of our favorites. He plodded to the reception counter and stared up at us with big, sad eyes and waited for us to come around to his side and pet him. We did, and he rolled over on his back and accepted our tummy rubs.

"I thought I'd better board him for a couple of days. The missus is on an Alaskan cruise with her girlfriends and with the murder and the wedding, who knows when I'll be able to get home."

"You ready to have some fun, Wally?" Josie said, stroking the dog's floppy ears. "You ready to go see all your buddies?"

We all laughed when he rolled over and headed straight for the back of the Inn toward his usual condo.

"Thanks a lot, Wally," Chief Abrams said, laughing and shaking his head as the basset disappeared from view. "I don't even get a goodbye?"

"He knows what he wants," Josie said, getting to her feet. "You look tired."

"Yeah, I was talking with the state cops until around two," he said, helping himself to a cup of coffee.

"Any update?" I said, holding my cup out for a top-up.

"Not really. They sort of like Jill's mom for it. But I'm leaning toward her sister. She's a piece of work."

"She was here with Jill earlier," I said, sitting back down behind the counter. "Why do you think she killed him?"

"She just seems capable of doing something like that and then not showing any remorse," he said, taking a sip of coffee.

"Or feeling any," Josie said.

"Yeah, that too," the Chief said, glancing out the window. "But nobody saw anyone messing around with the champagne glasses."

"Then it had to be somebody who was sitting right next to him, right?" I said.

"That's the only thing that makes any sense. Either that, or we're going to have to start suspecting one of your staff," the Chief said, chuckling.

"No, it wasn't anybody who works for us," Josie said. "If they were going to poison anybody, it would have been Beelzebub."

"Are they going to arrest Jill's mother?" I said.

"We talked about it a long time," the Chief said. "But we decided to hold off for now. We're going to keep a close eye on her at the wedding and reception to see if she tips her hand. I don't know," he said, shaking his head. "I just don't see her doing it."

"Well, there were fifty people around that table," I said. "Somebody could have easily walked by and dropped a little poison into the glass, right?"

"Sure. Everybody was eating and chatting with each other," he said. "It certainly wasn't impossible to pull that off. But how the heck could they be sure he'd be the one who ended up with that glass?"

"Which leads you back to the idea that the poison might have been meant for the mother," I said.

"Yeah, it's a strange one," the Chief said, glancing out the window. "Well, would you look at this."

He walked to the front door and held it open. Soon, three Labrador retrievers, no more than five months old, strolled inside like they owned the place.

"My goodness," Josie gushed. "They're gorgeous."

She knelt down, and all three dogs surrounded her, tongues licking and tails wagging. I sat down on the floor next to her, and the chocolate lab made a beeline for me.

"If you're not careful, you'll be down there all day with them."

All three of us looked at the woman who was standing in the doorway beaming at us.

"You must be Suzy and Josie," she said, strolling toward us. "Jill has told me so much about you."

"You're her godmother, right?" I said, climbing to my feet to shake hands. "Suzy Chandler. It's so nice to meet you."

"Missy McNamara," she said, returning the handshake. "And you must be Josie."

"Hi. Nice to meet you," Josie said, laughing as the two other labs did their best to keep her sitting on the floor. "When we heard you were bringing in three small dogs, we weren't expecting these guys. They're adorable."

"Yes, they certainly are," she said, beaming at the dogs. "And they're not going to be small much longer. Allow me to introduce you. The chocolate's name is Cocoa. The black lab is Licorice. And the yellow is Sunset."

"Three puppies are quite a handful," I said, rubbing the chocolate lab's head.

"Everyone thought I was crazy," Missy said. "But they've been inseparable almost since birth, and I couldn't bear to break them up. So, I just decided I had to get all three."

"Oh, no," Josie said, laughing. "Not the briar patch."

"Exactly," Missy said, glancing over at Chief Abrams and extending her hand. "I'm Missy."

"Chief Abrams. It's nice to meet you," he said, then his voice softened. "I'm so sorry for your loss."

I'd been so distracted by the arrival of the labs that I'd completely forgotten the woman was the ex-wife of the man who'd been murdered last night. But judging from the look on her face, it was pretty clear she didn't have a clue what Chief Abrams was talking about.

"My loss?" she said, frowning.

"You haven't heard," he said, embarrassed. "I'm sorry. I just thought you would have by now. I shouldn't have made the assumption."

"I think I'm going to need an explanation," she said, glancing around at our expressions.

"Haven't you talked with anyone yet?" I said.

"I've had my phone off since I left New Hampshire yesterday. I spent most of my week on the phone and decided to leave it off for a few days. And the silence has been a most welcome change."

"You might want to check your messages," I whispered.

She frowned at me but reached into her purse and removed her phone. She turned it on and waited. Then she grimaced and glanced around at us again. "Twenty-seven messages? What on earth is going on?"

She punched a few keys, then held the phone up to her ear and listened to the first message. Then she staggered backward and dropped the phone on the floor. The dogs were startled by the clatter, then noticed Missy's distress and trotted toward her. We helped her into a chair and stood by helplessly as she began to cry. Josie handed her some tissues, and we waited out the first of what I assumed would be several rounds of tears.

"Roger's dead? How did it happen?" she said, glancing up at Chief Abrams.

"We're still waiting for the toxicology report, but we think he was poisoned."

"Poisoned? What?"

"It appears something was put in his glass of champagne," I said softly. "At the rehearsal dinner."

"What on earth was he doing here at the wedding?" she said, baffled.

"Why does that surprise you?" Chief Abrams said.

"Because of all the bad history, primarily," she said through another burst of tears. "Has Jill told you the story?"

"Some of it," I said. "She said that your ex and her mom had a thing going on that was the major cause of both marriages breaking up."

"It was," Missy said, nodding. "By the time their affair ended, it was too late to salvage either one."

"Uh, the affair ended?" Chief Abrams said, glancing at me.

"Yes, several years ago," Missy said. "Why do you ask?"

"Because your ex-husband was invited to the wedding by Jill's mom," I said. "And from what we saw, it didn't look like the affair was over."

"Really? They were back together? That's impossible," she said, shaking her head. "They ended up hating each other. In fact, all four of us ended up hating each other."

"I don't know what to say, Missy," I said, shrugging. "They were getting pretty snuggly at dinner."

"Knowing her, it was probably just a ruse to get him to lower his guard," she said, then glanced at Chief Abram. "Is she a suspect?"

"I really shouldn't talk about it," he said.

"She has to be a suspect," Missy said, frowning. "Either her or that despicable creature she calls her daughter."

"I take it you're not a big fan of Faith," I said.

"Nothing gets past you," Josie whispered.

"Shut it."

"Have you met Faith?" Missy said.

"We have," I said.

"And?"

"And your contempt is completely understandable," I said, shrugging. "But murder is something else altogether."

"Did you know she was sleeping with Roger?" Missy said, wiping her eyes.

"Yes, we heard," I said.

"And she confirmed it herself last night when I interviewed her," Chief Abrams said.

"It's disgusting, but knowing both of them, I can't say I was surprised when Jill told me."

"When was that?" Chief Abrams said.

"When did she tell me?" Missy said, frowning. "It must be several months ago."

"So, they'd been an item for a while?" the Chief said.

"Apparently. But I haven't spoken to either one of them in a very long time. And I doubt if they were actually an item. It was probably a casual sort of thing where they got together when they didn't have anything better to do."

"Romantic," Josie said.

"If you knew them very well, their approach wouldn't surprise you at all," Missy said, tearing up again. She took several deep breaths and exhaled loudly. "Okay, I guess I should go touch base with some people." She exhaled again. "I am not looking forward to this." Then she snapped to attention. "How is Jill doing?"

"She's going to be okay," I said.

"The poor thing. I hate the fact that she has to deal with this right before her wedding. Do you know where she is at the moment?"

"I think her and Faith are running some errands," I said.

"Then I think I'll wait until later," Missy said, grabbing a piece of paper from her purse. "Could you give me directions to my hotel?"

Josie nudged me with her elbow, and I glanced over at her. She nodded her head in the direction of our house behind the Inn, and I smiled.

"If you don't feel like staying in a hotel, Missy, we'd be delighted to have you stay with us," I said. "We have a ton of room at the house."

"Really?" she said, giving it some thought. "Are you sure I wouldn't be imposing?"

"Not at all," Josie said. "But you will have to agree to do one thing."

"What's that?"

"You have to bring these guys with you," Josie said, leaning down to pet the black lab that had taken a keen interest in one of her shoelaces.

"Absolutely. You won't have to stay in a strange hotel, Chef Claire is making a lasagna that's a total knee-buckler, and you wouldn't have to leave these guys down here on their own."

"That does sound pretty good," Missy said, managing a small smile.

"Chef Claire is making lasagna?" Chief Abrams said, doing his best to sound casual.

"She is," I said. "Would you like to come to dinner, Chief?"

"I thought you'd never ask."

Chapter 5

Josie and I, wearing identical burgundy, floor-length, off the shoulder bridesmaid dresses, managed to get out of the car without snagging chiffon or dragging the bottom hem through the remnants of the morning's rain shower. My mother and Chef Claire were already waiting for us at the bottom of the steps that led into the church. They both beamed at us as we approached.

"You two look fantastic," my mother said, brushing away some imaginary lint from my dress. "Now, this is the way to dress, darling."

"Yeah, I'll make sure I wear it the next time I go fishing, Mom," I said, gently swatting her hand away.

"How is this memorial service supposed to work?" Chef Claire said, frowning. "I mean, are you guys expected to be there? I can't imagine you and the bride would be sitting there in your dresses the whole time."

"According to Jill, the bridal party is supposed to wait in the room off the back of the vestibule until the memorial service is over. Then we'll line up and get the ceremony started," I said.

"Who on earth decided to combine a memorial service with the wedding?" my mother said, frowning.

"Jill's mom," Josie said.

"Hmmm," my mother said.

"What is it, Mom?"

"It just seems a bit strange that the woman who's one of the primary suspects would feel the need to organize a memorial service for the victim."

"Maybe she did it to help cover her tracks," I said, shrugging. "You know, deflect attention away from her."

"I think it's weird," Chef Claire said.

"That's a word for it," my mother said.

"Apparently, it's not going to last long. Just a couple of people are going to say a few words," I said. "But pay close attention. Since we won't be there, I want to make sure we don't miss anything juicy."

"Maybe the killer will confess," my mother said, grinning at me. "Wouldn't that just frost your cupcakes if you weren't there to hear it?"

"You know me so well," I said, making a face at her before turning to Josie. "You ready?"

"Let's do this," she said, heading up the steps. "My feet are killing me already."

"Don't start. We can take our shoes off at the reception."

"Darling?"

"Yes, Mom?"

"You're about to enter a place of worship," she said, her voice rising a notch. "Please try to remember that. Let's not have any shenanigans today, okay?"

"Have a little faith, Mom," I said, laughing at my own joke.

We entered the church, and I spotted Rooster and Jackson standing just inside the vestibule. As the two groomsmen, they were wearing tuxedos and looking very dapper. Rooster, someone who took great pride in his usual disheveled look, had even gotten a haircut. And if I didn't know him as a man who spent most of his time wearing jeans and a sweatshirt usually streaked with engine grease, and an old pair of work boots sans shoelaces and socks, he could have easily been mistaken for some sort of corporate executive. Jackson, our former chief of police, and now the owner of our local grocery store, was tugging at his bow tie.

"Wow. You guys look great," Rooster said, immediately ushering us toward a door. "We're under strict orders to escort you right into the waiting room."

"Ordered by whom?" Josie said.

"Take a wild guess," Jackson said.

"Great. What sort of mood is Beelzebub in today?" Josie said.

"Let's call it demanding and leave it at that," Rooster said. "But you need to get in there and get your instructions."

"We just finished getting ours," Jackson said, shaking his head. "Oh, she made another slight change. Josie, now you're walking down the aisle with me."

"That means you're stuck with me, Suzy," Rooster said, laughing as he opened the door. "You two have fun."

We stepped inside and saw Jill looking resplendent in her wedding dress pacing back and forth. Faith stared at us and gave our outfits the once over. She frowned.

"What?" Josie said.

"Your hair."

"What about it?"

"You're both wearing it up."

"Nothing gets past you," Josie said, glaring at her.

"I'd prefer it if you wore it down," Faith said, putting her hands on her hips.

"And I wish you'd shaved yours," Josie said. "So, let's call it even."

"Okay, guys," I said, stepping in between them. "Cool your jets. We've got a long day ahead of us." I approached Jill and gave her a long hug. "You look fantastic. How are you holding up?"

"I'm a little nervous," she said, wringing her hands.

"You just relax and leave everything to me," Faith said, finally breaking eye contact with Josie. "Now that you're both *finally* here, we can go over how this is going to work." She pointed at three chairs sitting in a row along one wall. "Have a seat."

"Yes, Commander," Josie said, giving her a mock salute.

"I have to say that your attitude sucks," Faith said.

"Oh, good. That's what I was going for."

"Knock it off," I snapped. "Let's try to remember whose day this is."

"Thank you," Faith said, nodding at me.

"I was referring to Jill," I said, shaking my head.

"Oh, of course," Faith said, her face turning red. "Absolutely." Then she recovered and consulted her list. "Item one. As soon as the memorial service is over, the processional will begin. Personally, I think the song choice leaves a lot to be desired."

"What did you finally decide on?" I said to Jill.

"Here Comes the Sun," Jill said. "I couldn't bear the thought of Here Comes the Bride."

"Good compromise," I said, shrugging.

"Nice," Josie said.

"I had to fight Sammy pretty hard on that one," Jill said, laughing. "He wanted to do something funny to lighten the mood."

"What song did he want?" I said.

"Highway to Hell."

"AC/DC?" Josie said, laughing.

"Yeah," Jill said, shaking her head.

"That is pretty funny," Josie said.

"It's ridiculous," Faith said, then pointed at Josie. "You'll be walking down the aisle with that Jackson guy. He seems to be a bit of a lumberer, so don't let him dawdle."

"Got it. No dawdling with the lumberer."

"And Suzy will be walking with Rooster. What an odd name. But he seems like an odd man, so maybe it's appropriate."

"Where do we go once we make it down the aisle?" I said.

"You never listen," Josie said, shaking her head.

"Shut it."

"You'll both be sitting in the front pew on the bride's side during the Mass."

"Do we have to do the whole sit, stand, kneel thing?" I said, frowning.

"Of course," Faith said.

"Just follow my lead," Josie said.

"I always get confused," I said, scowling.

That was true. I did. After all those childhood years, the mass rituals should have been second nature to me, but my subconscious had created some form of mental block. But I knew I'd probably be able to make it through the service without embarrassing myself if I copied Josie. I just hoped I'd be able to be convincing in this dress. Shrink-wrapped and floor-length probably wasn't the best outfit for the well-executed sit, stand, and kneel routine.

"Well, if you'll excuse me," Faith said, draping a large shawl over her shoulders, "I need to get out there."

"Where are you going?" Josie said.

"To the memorial service. Where else would I be going?"

"In the immortal words of AC/DC-"

"Josie, that's enough," I snapped.

"Given my history with Roger, it's only appropriate that I should say a few words," Faith said, heading for the door. "I just hope this shawl covers enough of my dress. I want people to be surprised when they see me walking down the aisle later." She opened the door, then paused to look back. "Just wait here until I get back."

"Jill?" Josie said, staring at the now closed door.

"Yeah?"

"Are you sure she's really your sister?"

"She's a piece of work all right," Jill said, starting to pace the room again. "But my mom has been absolutely no help since we got engaged, and when Faith volunteered to be my maid of honor, I couldn't come up with a good reason to say no."

"Are you sure you're okay?" I said.

"I'll be fine," she said. "I'd just like to get this over with."

I felt a wave of sympathy wash over me. The poor woman should be experiencing one of the happiest days of her life, but she was dealing with a dead guy who'd been sleeping with both her mom and sister and been poisoned during her rehearsal dinner. Now, her special day had been temporarily delayed by a memorial service organized by her mother.

Note to self. Never mix weddings and memorial services.

"Hang in there," I said, patting her hand. "We'll help you get through this. And it's going to be great."

"I should be out there," Jill said, staring forlornly at the door. "I've known Roger pretty much my whole life."

"Beelzebub would have a coronary," Josie said, then held her hands out and urged us on. "C'mon, let's put our thinking caps on. There must be a way we can pull that off."

Jill and I both laughed. Then I noticed another door on the far side of the room and a memory popped to the surface.

"Hey, I've got an idea," I said, heading for the door. "Follow me."

"Where on earth are you going?" Josie said.

"That door leads to a set of stairs that go up to the choir loft. We should be able to watch the memorial service from up there without anybody noticing."

We slowly made our way up the stairs, and when we reached the top step, all two-dozen of the choir members, wearing robes and sitting quietly watching the memorial service play out below, turned their heads and stared at us. Millie, our new head bartender and a member of the choir, frowned at our surprise pop-in.

"What the heck are you guys doing up here?" Millie said.

"Shhhh," several choir members whispered.

"Sorry," I said, glancing around. "We just wanted to check out the service."

"There's no place for you to sit," Millie whispered.

"Shhhh."

I confirmed that there weren't any empty chairs and nodded at Josie and Jill to again follow my lead. I knelt down in front of the first row of chairs and peered over the top of the railing. My dress protested in the strongest terms possible, and being on my knees was an incredibly uncomfortable position, but the view of the church that stretched out below was perfect. Josie and Jill knelt beside me, and we ignored the disapproving titters of various choir members who sat behind us.

"Great dress," Millie whispered.

"Thanks," I said, glancing over my shoulder.

"I was talking to Jill."

"Oh. Sure, sure."

"Shhhh."

I focused on the front of the church where Jill's mother was making short work of a quasi-emotional tribute to Roger. Her tears seemed forced, as did the catch in her throat that surfaced every few seconds. I glanced over at Jill who was watching her mother's performance closely.

"How close was your mother to Roger?" I whispered to Jill.

"That depends on what time of day you're referring to," Jill whispered, glancing over at me.

"What?"

"Think about it," Josie whispered.

"Oh. Got it," I said, refocusing on her mother.

"Gentle and loving soul? What a piece of work," Jill said, disgusted. "Too bad she never uses those terms to describe the living."

I glanced over at her again and couldn't miss her scowl of contempt.

"Okay, she's done," Jill said, arching her back. "Can we get out of here?"

"No, let's give it a minute. I want to see what the Princess of Darkness has to say," I whispered. Then I caught myself and nudged Jill with an elbow. "Sorry. I shouldn't be talking about your sister that way."

"Knock yourself out," Jill said with a casual shrug. "You should hear what Sammy calls her."

Faith approached the podium that had been set up for the memorial service, and it was impossible to miss the fact that she and her mother barely acknowledged each other's presence when their paths crossed. Faith adjusted the microphone then launched into a tearful tribute that was even more saccharine that her mother's. Just as she was starting to tell a story about a moonlit night she and the deceased had spent together on a deserted beach, one of my calves began to cramp. I flinched and gripped the railing in front of me with both hands.

"What's the matter?" Josie said, giving me the once-over.

"Leg cramp," I said, grimacing. "Geez, that hurts." I attempted to reach back to massage my leg, but my dress stopped me short. "Oh, my leg is killing me."

"Shhhh."

"Shut it," I snapped, glancing over my shoulder at one of the choir members.

"Are you okay?" Jill said.

"Shhhh."

"I heard you the first time." I grimaced as I continued to reach behind me in an attempt to grab the fully-constricted muscle. "Ow, that's brutal." I grimaced as I continued trying to get a hand on my calf, then I lost my balance and toppled over on my side. Trapped by the tight gown, I flopped on the floor as I tried to get back into an upright position. I was sure I looked like a hooked fish flopping on the deck of my boat, and Millie and several other choir members were unable to stifle their laughter.

"Smooth," Josie said, laughing.

"I said, shut it. Now, help me up."

Josie and Jill got to their feet and helped pull me upright. I managed to stand, staggered momentarily on my heels, then looked out at the church below. The attendees were all turned in their seats and staring up at the choir loft. I made eye contact with my mother who was giving me a sad, angry shake of her head, then I noticed Faith gripping the lectern with both hands and giving me the death-stare.

"Sorry," I said to the crowd down below with a shrug. "Leg cramp."

Josie and Jill each grabbed an elbow and led me to the stairs. We made our way down the steps and back into the waiting room. I sat down on a chair and flexed my toes toward my head as far as I could and massaged the back of my calf.

"Now, that was funny," Jill said, sitting down and letting loose with a manic cackle that continued until Josie and I stared at her. Jill glanced back and forth at us. "I think I've hit the wall. Thanks, Suzy. I needed that." She wiped her eyes with a tissue and sat back in her chair with her legs splayed.

Seconds later, the door opened, and Faith stormed into the waiting room, closely followed by my mother.

"Are you purposely trying to ruin the day?" Faith said, glaring at her sister. "That was disgraceful. Not to mention incredibly disrespectful to Roger's memory. And don't sit like that. You're going to wrinkle your dress."

"Oh, stuff a sock in it," Jill said, waving her sister away.

"What? How dare you speak to me like that."

"Why don't you do all of us a big favor and just shut your mouth?" Josie said.

"Why don't you come over here and make me?" Faith said.

"Come over there and make you? What are you? Three?" Josie said, glaring back at her.

"Darling, what on earth is the matter with you?"

"I'm fine, Mom," I said, massaging my calf. "It's just a little leg cramp."

"Forget your leg. It's your brain cramp I'm worried about," my mother said. "What is it with you and churches? Every time you step inside this place, it's like you become obsessed with embarrassing me."

"Dial it down, Mom. I'm in serious pain here."

"Pain? I'll give you pain."

My mother's voice had deepened, and I was now officially in the danger zone and about ten seconds away from getting the dreaded, *young lady*.

"I've about had it with you," Faith said, taking a step toward Josie.

"People, please," Jill said. "I'm trying to get married here."

"Just leave everything to me, Jill. I've got this one," her sister said, taking a step toward Josie. "You want a piece of me?"

"Be still my beating heart," Josie said, slipping off her shoes and planting both feet firmly on the floor. "Bring it on, Beelzebub."

"I hope they have a wheelchair handy," Faith said, raising her fists. "Because that's the only way you're gonna make it down the aisle."

Faith's mistake was to lunge too early. She swung wildly and missed Josie by a foot. Faith's momentum carried her forward, off-balance, and Josie took full advantage. She fired a punch that caught Faith right across the bridge of her nose, and she went down hard. Blood starting spurting from her nose, and she grabbed it with both hands, glanced down at the mess, then screamed and swept a leg toward Josie who toppled over with a loud grunt. Faith pounced on Josie, and they wrestled on the floor until Josie managed to get an arm free and hammered Faith again. This time, the punch landed on the side of her head, and the maid of honor ended up on her back, eyes closed, blood streaming down her face, and breathing through her mouth.

"Enough!" Jill shouted.

Josie climbed to her feet massaging her hand and gave Jill a sheepish grin.

"Sorry," Josie said. "But she had it coming."

"Stop. Please, all of you, just stop," Jill said, leaning down to help her sister to her feet. "C'mon, get up. Geez, what a mess. You better not bleed all over my dress."

"Are you okay, dear?" my mother said to Josie.

"I'm fine," she said, rubbing her knee.

"I wish I could say the same for your dress," my mother said, pointing at a large tear.

Josie glanced down and noticed that her dress had torn away and was hanging off her waist.

"Ah, nuts," Josie said, glaring at Faith who was still bleeding profusely. "Now look what you've done."

"That's a lovely bra, dear," my mother said. "La Perla?"

"As a matter of fact, it is, Mrs. C.," Josie said, pulling her dress up.

"I have the same one in blue," my mother said.

"It's really comfortable."

"It certainly is. It's almost like you're not wearing one," my mother said, nodding.

"Okay, guys," I said, shaking my head. "Let's say we hold off on the fashion chat for a while. Jill, why don't you go get Faith cleaned up, and I'll deal with Godzilla here. Mom, can you go see if you can find a sewing kit somewhere?"

"All right, darling," she said, giving me another scowl. "But we're not done with this conversation."

"I'd be shocked if we were," I said, shooing her out of the room.

Jill led the wobbly Faith to the bathroom, and I stared at Josie who was standing still and holding her dress up with both hands.

"What?" Josie said.

"Good punch," I said, grinning.

"Which one?"

"Well, both of them. But the first one was my favorite."

"Yeah, me too. That second one hurt," she said, then frowned. "We're going to have to figure out some way to make it up to Jill."

"We? You're the one that punched the maid of honor."

"Yeah, but if you hadn't gotten that stupid leg cramp, we wouldn't be in this mess in the first place."

"So, now it's my fault?"

"That's the way I see it."

"Nice try," I said, making a face at her. "Do you think her eyes are going to turn black before we get through the photo sessions?"

"We can only hope."

Chapter 6

Faith got her wish.

To say that the people on both sides of the church were surprised by her walk down the aisle would be a major understatement. But her plan to present herself as some sort of royal princess, not to mention the real star of the show, failed miserably given the fact that she was limping badly and her nose was packed with tissues. Dark semi-circles were already beginning to form under both eyes. In the end, she'd decided to wear the shawl she'd worn to the memorial service. She was furious about having to make the concession since the shawl covered her shoulders and the cleavage she'd wanted to put on full display, but the bloodstains that covered the top portion of her dress had forced her hand. She reached the altar and did her best to appear regal as she climbed the small set of marble steps then stood staring out at the throng. She held her bouquet high, then spied Josie making her way toward her.

Faith continued to glare as Jackson slowly led the limping Josie down the aisle. While the maid of honor had definitely gotten the worst of it, the kick she'd taken Josie down with had left a nasty bruise just below Josie's knee. My mother and I had managed to reconstruct the front of her dress, but from the back, the dress looked like it had gone through the spin cycle with her wearing it, and two of the safety pins we'd been forced to use reflected in the light. Josie made it to the front pew, glared at Faith who was gently pressing the side of her nose to test for blood, then winced when she turned to watch Rooster and I coming down the aisle. Still dealing with intermittent leg cramps, I wobbled my way toward the first row of pews clutching Rooster's arm. Halfway down the aisle, Rooster glanced over at me, concerned.

"Have you been drinking?" he whispered.

"Leg cramp."

"You want me to carry you?"

"Funny."

My long journey finally ended, and Rooster patted my hand before heading to his pew directly across from us. Faith continued to stand in front of a chair next to the altar but was now shooting daggers at the best man who was unable to stop grinning at her face. Next to him was Sammy, who seemed baffled by Faith's appearance as well as our noticeable limps. But a huge grin appeared on his face when he spotted Jill making her way down the aisle.

Finally, a little bride and groom action to take our minds off what had transpired.

The mass was reasonably short, and I made it through with only minor cramping, most notably during the kneeling portion of the program. Then Josie and I, along with Rooster and Jackson, took our places on the altar next to the bride and groom. I wormed my way in between Josie and Faith, hoping to avoid a rematch during the ceremony, and beamed at the happy couple the entire time.

At least two people were happy today. And I was glad those two were Sammy and Jill. The hardest part of the day was over for them as soon as the priest pronounced them man and wife, and they headed down the aisle arm in arm and out of the church. Rooster extended his arm, and we followed Faith and the best man outside where the photographer was already trying to organize various groups of people. I spotted Faith consulting with the makeup artist who had arrived with the photographer. She carefully removed the wads of tissue from her nose and again checked to make sure the bleeding had stopped. Then the makeup artist applied several layers of what I assumed was a concealing agent.

Josie and I waited with Rooster and Jackson just outside the church and watched Sammy and Jill greet several well-wishers. Jill eventually spotted us, and she strolled over.

"Congratulations," I said, hugging her tight. "You made it through."

"Thanks," Jill said, returning the hug. "Slight change of plans. We're going to skip the wedding party receiving line. Faith isn't feeling up to it, so Sammy and I are going to handle it by ourselves." She looked over at Josie. "How's your leg?"

"It hurts," Josie said. "When will you need us for pictures?"

"It's going to be a few minutes before we start with the wedding party," Jill said, shaking her head. "Faith wants to do some solo maid of honor shots first. You know, before the bruises really start to show."

"Is she still planning on having them done in the garden?" I said, frowning.

"Yeah, she is," Jill said. "I tried to talk her out of it, but she won't listen."

"This I gotta see," Josie said, limping down the steps onto the path that led to the garden in back of the church. "C'mon, you don't want to miss this."

"I'll join you in a bit," Jill said, shaking her head. "But first I need to go grab my *husband*."

"Now, there is one happy woman," I said, watching her head in Sammy's direction.

"C'mon, hurry up," Josie said, nodding for me to follow her. "This is going to be good."

"Don't you think you're taking this a bit too far?"

"Not until she's wearing that shawl as a sling," Josie said, limping her way down the path.

We made our way to the garden where the photographer was already frowning and silently nodding at the myriad instructions Faith was giving him. The makeup artist was still working on her face, and she dabbed on a final layer of the concealer, then took a step back to review the results and shrugged.

"Okay, that's the best I can do," she said, standing next to the photographer.

"Faith," I said, unable to stop myself. "I don't this is a good idea."

"Like I'm going to take advice from you," Faith snapped.

She held the bottom of her dress up and inched her way into the garden that was bordered with a thicket of lilac in full bloom. After a few steps, she frowned and looked down at the ground.

"It's muddy in here," she said, shaking her head. "Unbelievable."

"Funny how that happens after it rains," Josie deadpanned.

"Try to stand on the stepping stones," I said, pointing.

Faith ignored us and continued to work her way into the garden until she was pleased with the background the lilac provided. She nodded at the photographer.

"Okay, let's get this going," Faith said, striking a pose. "How's this?"

"How about something a little less runway model?" the photographer said, lowering his camera. "Let's just start with a natural pose and go from there."

"Why is everyone fighting everything I'm trying to do?" she said, glaring at the photographer. "Just shoot the pictures, okay?"

"Okay, you're the boss."

Faith nodded and resumed her earlier pose. Then something buzzed her head, and she swatted at it with her hand.

"You probably don't want to do that, Faith," I said, watching the scene play out from a safe distance. "That's a yellowjacket, and it really hurts when they sting you."

"Yeah, you're just going to make him mad," Josie said, taking a step back.

Faith continued to swat at the bee that had now been joined by two of its friends. They circled her head, and she tried taking a step to one side, but the mud was making sudden movements difficult. Seconds later, it was impossible to tell whether Faith or the bees were more agitated as she flailed at them with both hands.

"Yellowjackets are the ones that can sting you multiple times, right?" Josie said.

"Yup. Please, come on out of there, Faith," I said, pleading with her. "You're going to get stung."

"Shut up," she snapped at me, then resumed waving both arms frantically as the bees increased the speed at which they were circling her head.

"Well, you gave it your best shot," Josie said, folding her arms across her chest as she watched the scene play out.

"Yeah, I did. But I guess she's a big girl and capable of making her own decisions."

"Pity they aren't *better* decisions."

"Yeah, good point," I said, taking another step back from the garden.

Josie glanced over at the photographer who was rapidly snapping pictures.

"I'm going to want a copy of those," Josie said, grinning at him.

"These are going to be great," he said, laughing.

The first bee stung her on the shoulder right through the shawl she was still wearing. Faith flinched and cried out, but it was the second sting on the bridge of her nose that really got her attention. Rather than think her way through the implications, she reacted on instinct and swatted the bee hard. Blood immediately began to spurt out of her nose. Enraged, Faith removed the shawl from her shoulders and snapped it like one would a wet towel at a playmate at the pool. The shawl didn't connect with any of the bees that continued to buzz her head in increasing numbers, but it did hit one of the lilac branches. Several dozen bees, their early afternoon snack interrupted, rose out of the lilac and headed straight for Faith. Realizing her mistake, Faith tried to make a hasty retreat, but her shoes protested and refused to follow. She came out of her Christian Louboutin stiletto pumps, stumbled a few steps forward, then fell face down in the mud.

The yellowjackets attacked in full force.

Faith screamed and wrapped both arms around her head.

The photographer's camera continued to click like a metronome.

The makeup artist stared down at the maid of honor laying in the mud and did her best not to laugh.

Josie and I looked on horrified by the assault Faith was receiving.

"We have to get her out of there," I said.

"And get stung like she is?" Josie said, frowning at me. "Not gonna happen."

"Hang on," I said, heading toward the back entrance of the church.

I did my best duck-waddle in my dress and covered the fifty feet as fast as I could and huffed and puffed my way through the back door. I glanced around, then spotted a fire extinguisher fastened to a wall. I grabbed it and hustled back to the garden where Faith was still under attack. I pulled the firing pin and pointed it at her.

"Shut your eyes, Faith," I said, raising the fire extinguisher.

"That's not gonna be a problem," Faith mumbled through a mouthful of mud.

I fired an extended stream of foam that soaked her and the bees. The bees that survived made a hasty retreat.

"Nice shot," Josie said, staring down at the foam-soaked Faith. "C'mon, let's drag her out of there."

We grabbed Faith by the shoulders, flipped her over, then helped her to her feet. We escorted her out of the garden then set her down gently on the lawn. She was sobbing hysterically and covered with welts.

"You're going to have to go to the emergency room, Faith," I said, grimacing at her neck and shoulders.

She managed a slow nod as her tears mixed with the blood that was still pouring out of her nose. Josie handed her a handful of tissues, and Faith glanced up then glared at Josie.

"Don't worry. You and I aren't done yet," Faith snapped, then flinched when she pressed the tissues against her nose.

"Tenacious little thing, isn't she?" Josie said.

"You gotta give her that."

"You can stop taking pictures now," Faith said, scowling.

"Just one more," the photographer said, focusing the camera. "C'mon, give me that same look again. Perfect."

Click.

Chapter 7

After Faith was taken to the ER, we continued with the photo sessions at the church, and the photographer did his best to work around the rather noticeable absence of the maid of honor. When we finished, Josie and I piled into a limo with the best man and Rooster and Jackson for the short ride to my mother's place where her backyard had been transformed into wedding reception central. A massive white tent filled most of the yard, and the tables were covered with white linen tablecloths. Rose and lily centerpieces provided the perfect accent, and there wasn't a lilac in sight.

My mother's attention to detail is matched only by her familiarity with the yellowjacket's fondness for the flower while in full bloom.

She greeted us upon arrival, and dozens of guests were already sitting at the tables enjoying cocktails and appetizers.

"You did a great job, Mom," I said, glancing around. "The place looks amazing."

"Thank you, darling," she said. "I approached it as a warm-up event for your wedding. Dare I dream."

"Here we go," Josie said, laughing.

"Not today, Mom. Okay?" I said, giving her a quick kiss on the cheek. "I'm ready for a glass of wine."

"How's the maid of honor doing?" my mother said.

"They're going to see what they can do about all the bee stings. But she got pounded. And they're going to try to get the swelling down around her nose and maybe reset it if it's broken. The paramedic said there's a chance she might be able to make it to the reception at some point." I glanced around again making a mental note of the people I wanted to speak with at some point in the festivities.

"Not today, darling," my mother said, noticing my wandering eyes and shaking her head.

"What are you talking about?"

"I know that look," she said. "You're about to go headfirst into snoop mode."

"This is probably going to be my only chance to talk to some of these people. And in case you forgot, there's a very good chance that the person who poisoned Roger is going to be here."

"Just promise me you'll try to take it easy," my mother said, placing a hand on my forearm. "Try not to annoy the guests."

"Sure, sure," I said, spotting Chief Abrams standing at the bar. "Save me a seat."

I headed for the Chief waving to several friends on the way. He was drinking a beer and chatting with the bartender.

"Hey, nice job," he said, turning toward me and leaning his back against the bar. "But what the heck happened?"

"Josie got into it with the maid of honor before the ceremony. She took a swing at Josie and missed. Then it kind of went downhill for her after that. For the record, she's a bit of a bleeder."

"So I noticed," the Chief said, taking a sip of beer. "Strange day. The first time I've ever been to a combination memorial service and wedding." He shook his head. "Strange."

"Indeed. You got any news?"

"Nothing really new," he said, taking another sip. "We should have the preliminary toxicology report back tomorrow. And the state police are still convinced Jill's mother had to be the one who slipped the poison into his glass." He frowned and stared off into the distance.

"But you're not convinced," I said.

"I'm not. Who knows, maybe the guy just had a heart attack."

"He didn't have a heart attack, Chief, and you know it," I said, making a face at him.

"But it just seems too easy," he said. "And why on earth would she do it at the table? She was sitting right next to him all night and would have known going in that she'd be the primary suspect."

"Yeah, that part of it does seem pretty cut and dried," I said, accepting the glass of wine the bartender was extending. "Thanks." I took a sip and set my glass down. "It's almost gift-wrapped."

"So, what's your plan for tonight?" he said, cocking his head at me.

"What makes you think I have a plan?"

"Let's call it a lucky guess."

"You know me so well," I said, grinning at him. "I was thinking about spending some time with some of Jill's family members as well as the other women Roger had been involved with."

"Funny, that's my plan as well," he said, finishing his beer. "But we better work separately. If we try to tag team anybody, they might get a little suspicious."

"Yeah, and we can annoy twice as many people that way," I said.

"You gotta play to your strengths, right? But let's get together later on to compare notes."

"Good idea," I said, nodding. "Who are you going to start with?"

"I thought I might start by offering my congratulations to Jill's parents," he said, nodding at the table they were sitting at. "Since they can't stand the sight of each other, maybe they'll be glad to have some company and feel like chatting."

"I like it," I said, nodding. "I'm going to have a talk with the two aunts."

"Which ones are they again?" the Chief said, glancing around.

"They're over there," I said, nodding at a nearby table. "The one on the far left is the sister of Jill's mom. The woman next to her is her dad's sister. Apparently, they both had torrid affairs with the deceased."

"That guy certainly got around," the Chief said. "The other woman at the table, Roger's ex. What's her name again?"

"Missy McNamara."

"Missy, that's it. Jill's godmother, right?"

"Yup, that's her. She's really nice."

"How long is she going to be staying with you?" the Chief said.

"A couple of days I think. She's never been up here before and wants to have a look around. And those are three of the most beautiful labs you'll ever see. They make me melt."

"Say no more," he said, laughing.

"You know what a soft touch we are when it comes to labs," I said.

"Yeah, it's only labs."

"*Especially* the labs. But Missy is great. You'll like her."

"Is she still grieving about her ex-husband?"

"I'd say sufficiently shocked. Sad, but way past grieving. They'd been divorced a long time."

"What does she do?"

"She's some sort of teacher I think. Maybe social studies," I said, frowning at my guess.

"Okay, I'll see you later," the Chief said, grabbing his fresh beer off the bar. "Happy hunting."

"You, too."

On my way to join Missy and the two aunts, I spotted Freddie heading my way waving an arm to get my attention.

"Where did you go?" I said to him. "You took off right after the ceremony."

"I had to stop by my office," he said. "The preliminary toxicology report came back early."

"That's great," I said, grabbing his arm and leading him to an empty table. We sat down next to each other, I leaned in close.

"Suzy, people will talk," he said, grinning at my proximity.

"Funny. What does the report say?"

"Well, like I said, it's only the preliminary report, but the deceased definitely ingested a lethal dose of cyanide."

"Is that all?" I said, staring at him.

"Geez, we're talking about cyanide here, Suzy. Don't you think that's enough?"

"What I mean is, did anything else show up in his system?"

"His dinner. He went with Italian. But they're still looking," Freddie said, shrugging. "The final report is probably going to take about a week. I need to go give the Chief an update."

"He said he was going to go congratulate Jill's parents," I said, my neurons starting to fire.

Freddie glanced around until he spotted the Chief. He stood up, still glancing around.

"Okay, got him. But I don't see Faith anywhere."

"Oh, that's right," I said. "You left right after the ceremony."

"Did I miss something?"

"Yeah, you might say that," I said, fighting back a smile as I recalled the sight of Faith flailing her arms at the bees.

"Well, I'm sure she's around somewhere. She's gorgeous. And I just love that cute little button nose she has."

"More like a clown nose at the moment," I whispered.

"What?"

"Nothing."

"We had a really nice time on the River the other night, but it was pretty cold out there. I thought the reception might be a good way to take things to the next level. If you know what I mean."

"Got it," I said. "But I don't like your chances, Freddie."

"Why not? Did she say something?"

"Not really," I said, shrugging. "But I doubt she's going to be in a romantic mood tonight."

"Like she's going to have a choice after I start working a little Freddie-magic on her," he said, tugging the lapels of his suit jacket and striking a pose.

"Freddie-magic?" I said, raising an eyebrow at him. "Really?"

"Too much?"

"Yeah, you might want to dial it down a bit," I said, laughing.

"And go for something more traditional, right?"

"You lost me, Freddie."

"You know, a little slow dancing. A couple glasses of champagne. Ask her to take a romantic stroll later on. Maybe I'll even pick some flowers for her from your mom's garden."

"Flowers?"

"Yeah. You guys love getting flowers, right?"

"Sure, sure. But a word of advice, if I were you, I'd stick with roses."

Chapter 8

Jill's aunts were pretty, friendly, and, given the fact they'd been pounding Kamikaze's since they'd arrived, extremely loud and chatty. They were constructing a pyramid of empty glasses on the table that was already three-levels high, and they weren't showing any sign of slowing down. A server arrived carrying six fresh cocktails, and he placed them down on the table in front of the two women. Jill's aunt, the sister of her mother, noticed me standing next to them at the table, beamed up at me, and pointed at an empty chair.

"Please, join us," she said. "Want a Kamikaze?"

"Uh, no, thanks," I said, holding up my wine glass. "But I will sit down. Hey, Missy."

"Hi, Suzy," Missy said, smiling at me as she noticed my caution about getting too close to the Kamikaze Kids. "Just stay on your side of the table, and you'll be fine."

"You're a real hoot, Missy." The woman turned to the other aunt, the sister of Jill's father. "Isn't she a hoot, Trudy?"

"I've always liked that about her," Trudy said with a glassy stare. "Are you sure you don't want one of these, Missy? They're delicious."

"Thanks, but I think I'll stick with the champagne," Missy said.

"Suzy?" Trudy said, squinting up at me. "I know you. You run the dog hotel Jill works at, right?"

"That's me," I said, smiling.

"Well, what do you know? Charlotte, this is Jill's boss." She grabbed two of the fresh drinks and handed one to her drinking companion. "You ready?"

"I'm ready," Charlotte said, raising her glass. "To Suzy."

"To Suzy."

They clinked glasses, tossed back their drinks, then carefully stacked the glasses on the pyramid.

"It's nice to finally meet you, Suzy," Trudy said, managing to avoid slurring by speaking very slowly. "I was going to introduce myself at dinner the other night, then Roger put a crimp in my plans."

"He sure did. But that's what he always did, right? Put a crimp in other people's plans," Charlotte said, then glanced at Missy. "No offense."

"Don't worry about it," Missy said, shrugging. "I'm just sorry I missed it."

Both of the aunts found her comment funny, and they roared with laughter. Then they each grabbed another drink and raised their glasses.

"To Roger," Charlotte said.

"To Roger," Trudy said. "May he rot in hell."

They tossed their drinks back, leaned forward and gently placed the glasses on the pyramid, then sat back in their chairs.

"Whew," Trudy said, exhaling. "We might want to slow down." Then she noticed my stare and blinked at me. "What?"

"I'm just trying to follow the thread," I said. "The Roger thread."

"If we're going to go down that road," Charlotte said, laughing. "I hope you brought something to write with."

"Oh, let's not spoil the party," Trudy said, waving it away. "Don't waste your time trying to figure all that out. He's not worth it. Uh, sorry, Missy."

"Don't worry about it," Missy said, casually taking a sip of champagne. "You two were sleeping with him long after I stopped."

"Yeah, I guess we were," Trudy said, then glanced over at Charlotte. "When did you stop?"

"Two years ago," she said, stifling a burp. "That was when he was getting all hot and heavy with the trollop."

"Faith?" I said.

"Well, I'm sure not talking about hope and charity," Charlotte said, then laughed loudly. "She gets her considerable trollop skills from her mother. My beloved sister."

"Should we drink to her?" Trudy said.

"My sister? Not a chance."

Trudy cracked up and reached for the two remaining Kamikazes. She handed one to Charlotte, and they clinked glasses.

"To the trollop," Trudy said, downing her drink.

"To the trollop."

"And the bees," Trudy said, cackling.

"So, Faith started sleeping with Roger right after your affair ended?" I said to Charlotte.

"No, I'm sure he started way before that," Charlotte said. "It ended right after I *caught* them together."

"Got it," I said, glancing at Trudy. "And you were sleeping with him before that?"

"Oh, way before. It must have been about three years after Missy kicked his sorry butt out." She glanced over at Missy. "Does that sound about right to you?"

"I wouldn't have a clue, Trudy," Missy said, seemingly unshaken by the conversation. "I was long gone by then."

"Well, you were smart," Charlotte said, then frowned. "Where did you go again?"

"I didn't go anywhere. I stayed in New Hampshire," Missy said, draining the last of her champagne.

"That's right," Charlotte said. "So, how's it going up there?"

"It's great."

"You still seem confused," Trudy said, staring at me.

"I'm just wondering how three women who had relationships with the same man could be having such a civil conversation," I said, frowning as I glanced back and forth at them.

"Misery loves company?" Missy said with a shrug.

That cracked Trudy and Charlotte up. Trudy scanned the table.

"I'd toast you for that one," she said to Missy. "But we're out of Kamikazes."

"Roger must have had something you all found appealing," I said.

"Yeah, he had his *talents*," Trudy said, grinning. "Unfortunately, they weren't enough by themselves."

"Exactly," Charlotte said. "Eventually, you had to talk to him."

"*That* was the problem," Trudy said, nodding.

I glanced at Missy who seemed to confirm what they were saying with a small shrug.

"But Jill's mom, your sister, seemed to be able to get past that," I said.

"Have you ever tried talking to my sister?" Charlotte said.

"Not really."

"Don't bother trying. She's about as interesting as this table. But I was curious when I heard she and Roger had started up again after all those years," Charlotte said, then looked at Missy. "I'm sorry, Missy. I know it's ancient history, but it's probably still painful."

"Like I said," Missy said, shaking her head. "Don't worry about it. Roger's affair with Jennifer is the least of my concerns."

"So, that is what ruined your marriage?" I said to Missy. "The fact that he slept with one of your friends?"

"Her *best* friend," Charlotte said.

"Yes, at the time I thought she was," Missy said, finally showing a bit of anger. "As it turned out, I suppose I should have thanked her. But, like you, I was curious about why the two of them reconnected. I thought they were done. Jill was always telling me how they couldn't even stand being in the same room together. I'm very surprised they were an item again."

"It's gotta be some weird competition with Faith," Charlotte said. "Those two have one seriously screwed up relationship."

"Yeah, I agree," Trudy said. "The mother discovers her daughter, a younger version of her, is trying to take her place with an ex-lover. I imagine that sent Jennifer into a tailspin."

"Oh, it did a lot more than that," Charlotte said. "She was furious. But Faith, being the determined little trollop she is, hung tough."

"And Roger reaped the benefits of having both women vying for his affections?" I said, casually.

"Yeah, I'm sure he did," Charlotte said. "They played right into his hands."

"This conversation is a complete waste of oxygen," Missy said, glancing up as a server carrying glasses of champagne approached. She grabbed one of the glasses, took a sip, then set the glass down.

The server held out the tray and Charlotte and Trudy both grabbed two glasses each. I waved the tray away.

"Oh, could you please bring us another round of Kamikazes?" Trudy said. "Six more oughta do it."

"Of course. Right away," the server said, bowing slightly.

I grinned when I saw him walk away shaking his head. Then my neurons flared and urged me to push the conversation along.

"It was just so horrible," I said, frowning. "I mean, what happened at the restaurant."

"Yeah, it kinda put a damper on the evening," Trudy said.

"I just can't imagine who could do something like that," I said. "If, of course, he was actually murdered. I suppose he could have had a heart attack."

Both Trudy and Charlotte snorted. They grinned at each other then glanced over at me.

"Don't you worry," Trudy said. "He was definitely murdered."

"You really think so?" I said.

"There's no doubt about it," Charlotte said. "And I don't think the cops are going to have to look too hard to figure out who did it."

"No, Charlotte, you're wrong," Trudy said. "I just don't think Jennifer could have done it."

"She was sitting right next to him at dinner," Charlotte said.

"And every time Faith left the dining room, he'd slip out of his chair and follow her," Trudy said. "One time he came back into the dining room, and I saw a look on Faith's face that sent chills through me. It had to be the trollop."

"Maybe they worked together on it," Missy said, then took a small sip of her champagne.

"Ooooh, a tag team murder," Charlotte said, raising her glass in Missy's direction. "I like it."

"Who do you think killed him?" Trudy said to Missy.

Missy thought about it for a moment, then shrugged as she stared at both women.

"Knowing what I know about Roger's scorecard, I'm sure there's a ton of possible suspects."

Both Trudy and Charlotte flinched, then quickly recovered and drained their champagne. They set their glasses down, picked up a fresh one, and made eye contact with each other before they clinked glasses and took another sip.

Their reaction was enough to get them on my list.

I looked down the table at Missy who seemed melancholy and drained by the conversation.

I imagine losing your ex-husband, despite whatever problems you had shared, was a traumatic experience, her protests to the contrary notwithstanding. But the fact that Jill's mother had once been her best friend, then had betrayed her in the most despicable manner possible, nagged at me.

And the idea that Josie or I would be capable of doing something like that to each other was unimaginable.

I glanced over at the table where Chief Abrams was still chatting with the estranged couple and decided it was time to drop in.

"Are you okay?" I said to Missy.

"I'll be fine," she said. "It's just that a lot of bad memories have resurfaced."

"I can only imagine," I said, giving her a sad smile. "Can I get you anything?"

"Actually," she said, nodding at Trudy and Charlotte. "I was thinking about having a Kamikaze."

Chapter 9

Jill's parents were in better shape than her two aunts, but not by much, and I was glad I stopped by when I did. They were making short work of the two magnums of champagne that sat in a large ice bucket on the table, and her father's eyes were on the prowl for signs of a server. I smiled at them, and they gestured for me to sit down. I took a seat next to Chief Abrams.

"Did Freddie find you?" I said to him.

"He did," the Chief said, nodding.

"I guess it confirms one piece of the puzzle," I whispered to him before glancing around the table with a big smile. "What are we talking about?"

"Bill here and I were just talking about ancient Rome. He's a history professor."

"Interesting," I said.

"Yes, I find it fascinating," Bill said, still on the lookout for a server.

Jennifer, his ex-wife, snorted, then refilled her champagne glass.

"That's our Bill, all right," she said. "Only interested in the old and decrepit."

"I don't know, Jennifer," Bill said, eyeing his ex-wife over the top of his champagne. "If that were the case, then you and I should have been soulmates forever."

Jennifer flinched and stared off into the distance through narrowed eyes but said nothing.

"Wow," I whispered. "Good shot."

"Just wait," the Chief whispered back. "You haven't seen anything yet." He focused on Bill who was grinning, obviously pleased with his most recent rejoinder. "You were saying something about how dinner the other night reminded you of ancient Rome."

"Yes, in Roman times, poison was one of the more popular methods used to eliminate rivals. And it was quite common for the poisoning to be carried out at the dinner table," Bill said, effortlessly sliding into his professor role. "I'm sure the substance used to kill Roger was quite different from the poisons back then, but the historical reference was impossible to miss." He took a big sip of champagne and glanced at his ex-wife. "Which leads me to my next question. What did you use to kill him, Jennifer?" He sat back and grinned at her.

"You're such a loser," she whispered.

"Now that I think about it," Bill said, cocking his head. "Maybe the poison was similar. According to legend, Nero's favorite poison was cyanide."

It was our turn to flinch, and I snuck a glance at the Chief.

"Did you mention cyanide to him?" I whispered.

"Of course not," he said, not taking his eyes off the professor.

"You think it's just a coincidence? Maybe a lucky guess?"

The Chief shrugged and continued to stare at the estranged couple.

"I can't even begin to count the ways I hate you," Jennifer said.

"I'm sure you recognize that strategy, Chief Abrams," Bill said.

"I'm sorry. I'm not following you," the Chief said, frowning.

"Her use of a simple statement of fact to redirect the conversation away and thereby avoid having to answer my question," Bill said, staring at her. "Well played, Snuggy." He glanced over at us. "That was Roger's nickname for her. Wasn't it, *Snuggy*?"

"You're such a disgusting pig," Jennifer said. "And let's not forget, you had a lot more reasons to kill him than I did."

"Yes, I suppose I did," Bill said, giving it some thought. Then he grinned at his ex-wife. "So, don't keep us in suspense, Snuggy, what did you use?"

Jennifer fired what was left of her champagne into her ex-husband's face, then casually refilled her glass. Bill slowly wiped his face with his napkin then tossed it on the table.

"Don't murderers often exhibit that same characteristic, Chief?" Bill said. "That sudden burst of unprovoked rage that leads them to do things they normally wouldn't."

"We must have a different definition of unprovoked," Chief Abrams said. "I'm sorry, Bill, but you sort of had that one coming."

"Oh, we're just getting warmed up, Chief Abrams," Bill said, chuckling. "Stick around for a while. I'm sure that soon Jennifer will be coming after me with a knife." He paused to savor a sip of champagne. "Either that, or she'll be dancing on the table naked."

"I've had enough of this," Jennifer said, getting to her feet. "I'm going to talk with the bride and groom."

We watched her storm off, then I focused on Bill who was toying with his glass deep in thought.

"Was that really necessary?" I said.

"Probably not," he said without looking up. "But since we haven't seen each other in a very long time, I figured one more walk down memory lane couldn't hurt. You know, for old-time sake."

"But it's your daughter's wedding day," I said, baffled.

"Yes, it is," he said, smiling. "And the ceremony was delightful. As is this reception." He raised his glass to me. "Thanks to you and your mother I'm told. She has a lovely home. To your health." He drained his glass and exhaled loudly.

I glanced at Chief Abrams, and he gave me a slight nod. I leaned forward and placed my elbows on the table.

"I'm so sorry about what happened between you and your ex-wife," I said. "But you don't really think she was capable of killing Roger, do you?"

"She was sitting next to him all during dinner."

"But that doesn't mean she put poison in his drink."

"No, it doesn't. But she had motive and opportunity," he said, giving me a crocodile smile that made me nervous. "All you need to do is identify the means. But I imagine you're hoping that the toxicology report gives you that, right, Chief Abrams?"

"The thought has crossed my mind," the Chief said, nodding.

"Of course, it has," he said, staring at the Chief. "Just like the thought that I might have been the one who killed him."

"That thought has also crossed my mind," the Chief said, smiling at him.

"My opportunity, giving the seating arrangement at dinner, was somewhat limited. But I will concede that Jennifer and I do share at least one motive."

"The fact that Roger was sleeping with your daughter," I said.

"That did bother me at first," he said. "But over the years, I've come to accept Faith's...proclivities. And when they got combined with Roger's base instincts and weaknesses, the results were inevitable. And incredibly toxic. But if my daughter and ex-wife willingly choose to lay down with creatures like that, so be it."

"So, what shared motive are you referring to?" the Chief said.

"The damage he did to our family," Bill said, shrugging. "And I was hoping to get the chance to remind him of that over the weekend. But I guess my chance to do that is now gone forever."

"Who do you think killed him? I mean, if we take Jennifer out of the mix," I said.

"I can think of several people," he said, getting up out of his chair. "But you only need to find the right one."

"That's how it usually works," the Chief said.

"I wish I could help you, Chief Abrams. But I'm afraid my expertise is limited to the study of history, not criminology. Now, if you'll excuse me, I think I'll take a stroll through your mother's lovely garden before it gets too dark. It was a pleasure chatting with you."

He waved over his shoulder as he walked away. I watched him go until he reached the edge of the garden and disappeared from view.

"What do you think?" Chief Abrams said.

"I don't like him."

"Personally? Or for the murder?"

"Personally," I said, glancing over at him. "I'm gonna go with a strong maybe for him being the killer."

"I like him."

"Personally?"

"Absolutely not," the Chief said, scowling. "He's a pompous buffoon."

"You like him because of the cyanide comment, right?"

"Yeah, that one just kinda slipped out. He seemed embarrassed right after he said it."

"He definitely let it slip," I said, nodding. "But I read it like he was trying to torment his ex-wife by saying that, not only does he know she did it, he knows *how* she did it."

"I think you're reading way too much into it."

"Yeah, probably. I really need to start working on that."

"And ruin your delightful personality?" he said, laughing. "Hey, it looks like they're getting ready to serve dinner. You getting hungry?"

"Finally. A question I can answer."

Chapter 10

I pushed my half-eaten dessert away and took a sip of coffee as I watched Sammy and Jill laugh and whisper in each other's ear. They were sitting by themselves at a table set for four, and I glanced around for signs of the best man who, given Faith's absence, must have felt like an intrusive third wheel during dinner. I spotted him sitting with members of Sammy's family, caught his eye and waved, then looked down when I felt my dessert plate brush against my hand. I looked over at Josie who had almost gotten away unscathed.

"It looked like you weren't going to eat it," she said, her fork poised.

"No, two and a half of those are my limit," I said, shaking my head. "Knock yourself out."

Chief Abrams, sitting to my left, leaned forward and stared at Josie as she made short work of my Amaretto-cream-filled brownie. It was one of our favorites, and Chef Claire had kindly offered the recipe to the people catering the reception. Maybe *kindly offered* is a bit of a stretch. Josie had badgered Chef Claire relentlessly and guilted her into turning it over by saying that, without the brownies, the reception would feel incomplete. I'm not sure about that, but I am glad Chef Claire finally folded. The brownies were a total knee-buckler.

"Where on earth do you find room?" Chief Abrams said.

Josie shrugged as she wiped her mouth then sat back in her chair.

"I'm just a little piggy," she said, gently patting her stomach then reaching for her coffee. She glanced over at us. "Did you two have any luck?"

"I've got a working theory and a whole bunch of unanswered questions," I said.

"I've got more than that," Chief Abrams said, laughing. "I've got a whole bunch of different theories."

"Do any of them hold water?" I said.

"Nah," he said, shaking his head. "They have their strong points, but they all share a common characteristic."

"Lack of tangible proof?" I said.

"You got it in one," Chief Abrams said. "The problem is, I can make a good case for several of them being the killer."

"Five of them, right?" I said, raising an eyebrow.

The Chief paused to count his potential suspects on his fingers then nodded.

"Yeah. The two aunts who are building the glass pyramid at their table, the maid of honor, and both of Jill's parents. That's five. Did I miss anybody?"

"No, that's my list."

"I'd add one more," Josie said casually as she grinned and waved to a small group of guests who were walking past our table.

"Who's that?" I said.

Josie pointed at a pretty young woman wearing a white blouse and black pants who was scurrying around the tables collecting dirty dishes.

"She works for the catering company," Chief Abrams said. "Why the heck would she kill the guy?"

"How the heck would she even know him?" I said, frowning.

"I was talking to her earlier," Josie said, waving to some more people. "She's a college kid who's spending the summer here. Bobby, the guy who owns the catering company, is apparently her uncle."

"And she somehow managed to fall under the spell of Roger during a dinner she wasn't even at, then had an epiphany and decided to poison him?"

"You didn't let me finish," Josie said, focusing on both of us. "Have a guess where she goes to college?"

"The Culinary Institute?" I said, frowning.

"Guess again," Josie said, shaking her head at me.

"How the heck would I know where she goes to school?"

"She goes to school in New Hampshire," Josie said.

"Geez, Josie, thanks for clearing that up," I said, turning to the Chief. "I guess we can wrap this one up. Mystery solved."

"You're not making the connection?" Josie said. "And just so we're clear, you can stop snarking at me anytime now."

"I'm not snarking," I said. "What connection?"

"College in New Hampshire. Two of her professors are here tonight. One of them is her *absolute favorite* in the whole world. Her term, not mine."

I sat quietly, deep in thought as I tried to make sense of what Josie was saying. I placed my elbows on the table, rubbed my temples, and waited for my neurons to fire. Eventually, some sparked and a lightbulb flickered.

"Jill's dad is one of her professors?" I said.

"Not just one of her professors," Josie said. "Her *favorite* professor."

"That's a really strange coincidence," I said, still frowning.

"It certainly is," Chief Abrams said. "She didn't happen to mention the names of any courses she's taken with him, did she?"

"She said she's only taken one so far," Josie said. "But she plans on taking all of them. The course she took last semester was called The Joys and Perils of the Roman Empire."

I stared at Chief Abrams, who seemed even more confused than I was.

"No way, right?" I said, frowning.

He shrugged and stared off into the distance deep in thought.

"Hang on," I said, glancing at Josie. "You said two of her professors were here. Who's the second one?"

"Really?" Josie said, raising an eyebrow at me.

"What?" I said, starting to get annoyed. "How the heck would I know who it is?"

"Probably because she's staying at the house with us," Josie said, shaking her head. "What did you do? Forget to pay your Snoopmeter bill?"

"Missy?"

"Nothing gets past you," Josie said, snorting.

"Shut it." I toyed with my water glass as I tried to process the information. "Missy's a professor? I thought she taught high school social studies."

"She's a Sociology professor," Josie said. "How much have you had to drink?"

"Obviously, not enough," I said. "How do you know she's a professor?"

"Oh, I don't know. Maybe because we spent a half-hour talking about it in the living room the other night."

"We did? What was I doing?"

"You were rolling around on the floor with the three puppies."

"Well, there you go," I said, shrugging. "That explains why I wasn't paying attention."

Josie rolled her eyes at me and removed a magnum of champagne from an ice bucket and poured three glasses. She took a sip of hers then her eyes drifted away. I followed her stare then nudged the Chief with my elbow.

"Interesting," he said, nodding.

103

"It looks like Jackson and Missy are going for a little nighttime stroll in your mom's garden," Josie said.

"Good for them," I said, my neurons still preoccupied. "Jill's dad and Missy are professors at the same college?"

"You are on fire tonight," Josie said, laughing.

"Shut it. But how did they end up teaching at the same college?"

"I must say that your ability to pay attention is somewhat situational," Josie said. "They've been teaching there forever. That's where they all met, remember?"

"How would I remember something I never knew in the first place?"

"She's got you there," the Chief said, laughing.

"Remind me to put the dogs outside the next time we're about to start a serious conversation," Josie said. "Jill's dad and Missy both got jobs at the university the same year. And the four of them were best friends for years."

"I remember the part about them being best friends," I said. "And after the divorce, Jill's mom took her and her sister and moved away?"

"She did," Josie said. "But Bill had tenure and wasn't going anywhere. And Roger's business was there, so he stayed."

"He'd been living in the same town with Bill and Missy all these years?"

"That would be my guess," Josie said, taking a sip of champagne.

"Now, I'm thoroughly confused," I said, shaking my head.

"Then my work here is done," Josie said, laughing as she stood up. "I'm going to go say goodbye to Sammy and Jill."

"Okay. Tell them I'll be over in a few minutes," I said, giving her a quick wave. Then I called after her. She turned around and headed back toward the table.

"What's up?"

"I was just wondering how you got into the conversation with the server," I said, looking up at her.

"She was walking around with a tray of the stuffed mushrooms earlier, and I mentioned how garlicky they were," Josie said. "She agreed, then offered me something."

"The rest of the tray?" I said.

"Funny. No, she offered me a breath mint."

"Really?" I said, then shrugged it off. "Lots of people use them. It's probably nothing."

"Didn't you say that the woman in the bathroom had made Roger eat a mint before agreeing to kiss him?" Josie said.

"I did. Are you inferring that the server might have also been involved with Roger?"

"I'm not inferring anything," Josie said. "That's your job. I just thought you might want to know."

A total neuron overload ensued. I frowned and rubbed my temples.

"Try not to overthink it," Josie said. "And don't forget to say goodbye to Sammy and Jill before they leave. They're heading up to Ottawa tonight and catching an early flight to Grand Cayman in the morning."

"I won't forget. See you in a bit."

"They're going to stay at your place down there?" the Chief said.

"Yeah, there was no reason for them to pay all that money to stay at a resort," I said, still distracted. "The house is empty."

"That was very nice of you guys to do that for them," he said.

"It was the least we could do," I said, waving it off. "None of this makes a lot of sense, Chief."

"Well, we have to assume that the server being here tonight is a total coincidence. There's no way that could have been planned."

"No, you're right, it couldn't," I said. "Do you think she and Bill could be an item?"

"A professor having an affair with one of his students? Sure, why not? It happens all the time."

"And if she was the woman in the bathroom with Roger, that would mean she was also getting busy with him."

"And cheating on Bill with the same guy who had an ongoing affair with his ex-wife."

"Which ruined his marriage," I said.

"Yup. Plenty of motive there," the Chief said.

"How hard is it to get your hands on cyanide?"

"Don't be discouraged, Suzy. I'm sure your love life will pick up soon."

"Funny."

"I'm sure you could find cyanide easy enough if you knew where to look," the Chief said. "You're starting to like Bill for it, right?"

"Yeah, I think I am.

"Me, too."

"There you are."

The Chief and I glanced up and saw Freddie approaching. He grabbed a chair and set it down between us. Neither one of us could miss the excited look on his face.

"I've been looking for you," Freddie said.

"What's up?" the Chief said.

"I just got another call from the lab," Freddie said, helping himself to a glass of champagne.

"At this hour?" I said, frowning.

"Yeah, the guy who got assigned the case is young and out to make a name for himself. As such, he's putting in a ton of hours, and this one really got his attention. You'll never guess what he found a couple of hours ago."

"I'm gonna guess it wasn't his car keys," the Chief said.

"Good one, Chief," Freddie said. "You really should have gone into stand-up. Anyway, he was just starting to do a little more panning for gold in the victim's GI tract."

"Geez, Freddie," I said, frowning. "We just ate."

"Well, excuse me. You want to hear this or not?"

"Go ahead," I said. "But try not to be too graphic."

"He found some cyanide," Freddie said, beaming as he glanced back and forth at us.

"Isn't that what he would expect to find?" the Chief said, frowning. "Especially since he already found some."

"Yes, he did find cyanide in the victim's stomach," Freddie said, then paused for effect. "But not in capsule form."

I sat back in my chair and waited out the explosion and subsequent collision of neurons. It took a while. Fortunately, the Chief had the same reaction. Freddie continued to grin at us as we collected our thoughts.

"Capsule form," I whispered.

"Yeah, he found a partially dissolved capsule with cyanide residue all over it."

"Now, there's a stroke of luck," Chief Abrams said.

"Why wouldn't the capsule have been completely dissolved?" I said.

"Stuff like that happens," Freddie said with a shrug. "I imagine the guy's system must have shut down before his gastric juices could finish their work. Apparently, he'd eaten a really big dinner. The guy at the lab said he found what was left of the capsule right in the middle of a bunch of undigested lasagna. He said it was nestled between a piece of Italian sausage and a chunk of mozzarella."

"Yuk," I said, grimacing.

"I guess we're lucky he didn't decide to have the consommé," the Chief deadpanned.

"Now, that's funny, Chief," Freddie said, laughing.

"Please, stop. Both of you," I said, rubbing my temples. I formulated my question, then glanced over at Freddie. "How long does it take for a capsule to dissolve and release its contents?"

"Fifteen to thirty minutes is the general rule of thumb. Plus or minus a few minutes on either side."

"So, it's possible that he was given the cyanide capsule before he sat back down at the table?" I said.

"Absolutely," Freddie said. "Maybe he was on some sort of prescription, and somebody switched the pills. If was used to taking them, he might not have even bothered looking at the pill before he swallowed it."

"No, that's not what happened," I said, flashing back to the time I was trapped in the bathroom closet.

"The men's bathroom," the Chief said, nodding.

"Yes. When I was in the bathroom, I specifically heard Roger say something about what a great kiss she'd given him. Then he laughed and said to whoever was in there with him that she'd shoved the breath mint right down his throat with her tongue."

"Why can't I meet a woman like that?" Freddie said, laughing.

"I think you might have already met her, Freddie," I said, staring at him.

"Faith? No. No way."

"She's certainly a distinct possibility," I said, glancing over at Chief. "Do you remember seeing anybody getting up from the table around that time?"

"Yeah, me," the Chief said. "I had to step out to take a call."

"Okay," I said, frowning. "Maybe my mom was there the whole time. I'll check with her."

"I was there," Freddie said. "But Jackson and I had a long talk during dinner. I wasn't paying much attention to who was coming and going."

"Putting a cyanide capsule in your mouth would be a pretty risky move," the Chief said. "If it got stuck in her mouth and dissolved before she could transfer it, she'd been the one getting her GI inspected at the moment."

"Maybe not if she put the capsule inside something else," I said.

"Like what?" Freddie said.

"I don't know. A piece of candy. Maybe gum. Something like that," I said, shrugging.

"That could work," the Chief said. "And it sounds like the mint was enough of a distraction. You said he choked a little on whatever he swallowed."

"Yeah, he did," I said. "But it was pretty clear he assumed it was the breath mint that got caught in his throat. Then he went back to the table to make his toast. Champagne has a high acidity, right?"

"It does," Freddie said. "You think that it might have been the champagne he drank during the toast that caused the capsule to pop in his stomach?"

"The thought did just cross my mind," I said, nodding.

"Mine, too," the Chief said. "What a perfect alibi. Man, if she managed to pull that off, we might be dealing with a very dangerous individual. That's diabolically brilliant."

"You really think Faith might have done it?" Freddie said.

"I have to say she's pretty high on my list," the Chief said.

"How friendly did the two of you get when you took her out on your boat the other night?" I said.

"Well, she certainly didn't try to shove anything down my throat," Freddie said, shrugging. "But she is a good kisser. I was hoping to see her here tonight."

"It looks like you might get your chance," I said, catching a glimpse of Faith walking across the lawn toward Sammy and Jill's table.

Faith was wearing jeans, a loose-fitting sweatshirt and a large pair of dark sunglasses. She continued to make her way to the table, then spotted Josie sitting with the happy couple and made a sharp right turn. After a few more steps, she stopped to glance around for a place to sit, then gave me a small wave and a made a beeline for our table.

"Mind if I join you?" she said, sitting down next to me.

"Hi, Faith," Freddie said.

"Oh, hi," she said, then glanced at the Chief. "You're the chief of police here, right?"

"I am. Nice to meet you."

"Yeah, whatever," she said, then nodded in Josie's general direction. "I want to file assault charges against that woman."

"I see," the Chief said.

Faith removed her sunglasses to reveal two very black eyes. Her nose was swollen to twice its normal size and apparently forcing her to breathe through her mouth. Freddie flinched when he got a good look at the damage and draped an arm over her shoulder.

"Get your hand off me," Faith said, jerking backward in her chair. "In case you forgot, I'm also dealing with dozens of bee stings."

"Bee stings?" Freddie said, puzzled.

"I wouldn't try to press charges, Faith," I said.

"And why not?" she snapped.

"Because I was an eyewitness. It was obvious that Josie was acting in self-defense. And I'm sure my mother and Jill will confirm it."

"Of course," Faith said, shaking her head. "All the local yokels are going to stick together." She grabbed her purse and began rummaging through it. "I need a cigarette."

She removed a set of keys and tossed them on the table as she continued to dig through her purse. She located a lighter, set it aside, then resumed her search. She tossed a container of breath mints on the table, then flicked a small, clear plastic bag containing three capsules next to them. Faith finally located her cigarettes, then lit one and sat back in her chair blowing smoke up into the cool night air. I glanced down at the bag, then looked at the Chief who was also staring at it.

"Uh, Faith," I said, casually.

"What?"

"What's in that bag?" I said.

"What bag?

"The little plastic bag on the table next to your mints," I said, pointing at it.

She glanced down at it, picked it up and examined it with both hands.

"I have no idea," she said with a blank stare. "Why don't you try one and let me know how it is?"

"Uh, thanks," I said. "But I think I'll pass."

She dropped the bag on the table, then sat back and focused on her cigarette. Soon, it was impossible for her to ignore the stares all three of us were giving her.

"What on earth is the matter with you people?" she snapped as she glanced back and forth at us.

The Chief removed a handkerchief from his pocket and wrapped the plastic bag in it.

"I think we need to have a little chat, Faith," the Chief said.

"Knock yourself out," she said, watching the Chief's movements.

"I think we should have this conversation down at the station," he said.

"I'm not going anywhere," she said, crushing out her cigarette.

"Well, I guess we're just going to have to disagree on that."

"You're joking, right? You're arresting me?"

"No, let's say that I'm going to be holding you," the Chief said.

"For what?"

"For questioning."

"For how long?"

"Not long. But you will need to stick around town until we get some lab results back regarding what's in those capsules."

"I've never seen that bag before," Faith said, her eyes starting to widen. "Somebody must have put those drugs in my purse."

"Drugs?" the Chief said. "What makes you think they're drugs?"

"What else would they be?" she said, now officially worried. "And for the record, I don't do drugs. It's probably some sort of painkiller. Or maybe it's Ecstasy."

"For your sake, I hope that's all it is," the Chief said.

"This is the worst day I've ever had," Faith said, shaking her head.

"For your sake," I said softly. "I sure hope so."

Chapter 11

After we said our goodbyes to Sammy and Jill, they headed off to begin their honeymoon. Then we said goodbye to my mother after the last of the guests had departed and headed home. We took quick showers, changed into tee shirts and sweats, then sat down in the living room to relax and play with the dogs who made it abundantly clear that they had missed us. Josie made a pot of coffee while I built a fire. Even though it was late May, the night had turned cold, and soon the dogs were stretched out in a row and sound asleep in front of the fire.

"This is nice," Missy said, her feet propped up on the footstool in front of her chair. "You guys do this all the time?"

"As often as we can," Chef Claire said, sipping her coffee.

"Do you think Faith is going to be charged with Roger's murder?" Missy said.

"If those pills have cyanide in them, it's almost certain," I said, stretching out on one of the couches.

Chloe woke up when she heard the familiar sound of me getting comfortable on what she considered her couch and was soon stretched out across my legs.

"Oh, I'm sorry," I said, glancing down at my Aussie. "Am I taking up too much room?" Chloe snorted but grudgingly conceded a bit more space. "There was a lot more room when you were a puppy."

"Speaking of puppies," Josie said, nodding at the three labs that were nestled up against Al and Dente, Chef Claire's Goldens. "How cute is that?"

"Before I got them, I couldn't imagine myself having three dogs," Missy said, staring at the sleeping dogs. "Now, I can't imagine living without them." She smiled then her expression turned into a small frown. "What were you saying about some sort of capsule being found in Roger's stomach?"

"Apparently, he was given the poison in a capsule form," I said, staring up at the ceiling. "I'd just assumed that whoever killed him put some drops in his glass of champagne."

"That would mean that he might have been given the poison before he came back to the table, right?"

"That's the new working theory," I said, then glanced over at Missy. "Do you think it's possible that Faith could do something like that?"

Missy scoffed, but then teared up and wiped them away with the back of her hand.

"Sadly, yes, I do. She's always been troubled. Even from a very young age. And when she learned what her mother and Roger had done, it had a major impact on her. They left New Hampshire shortly after that."

"And you work with Bill?" I said.

"Well, we teach at the same university, but rarely see each other," Missy said. "Our buildings are on opposite ends of the campus."

"And Roger lived in the same town, too?" I said, yawning.

"No, it wasn't the same town," she said, shaking her head. "It's only about fifteen miles away, but as far as Roger and I were concerned, it might as well have been a different planet."

"What did he do?"

"Apart from chase women?" she said, laughing. "He had a software company. He did very well."

"Who gets it now?" I said, sitting up. Chloe took advantage and stretched out to full-length. "You two never had any kids, and he never remarried."

"You know, that's a very good question," Missy said, frowning. "I have no idea who will inherit the business."

"That might be worth checking out," Josie said. Captain opened his eyes when he heard her voice, and he got up and joined her on the couch she was sitting on. She disappeared from view for a few seconds as he moved around searching for the perfect spot. "No, by all means, make yourself comfortable." Seconds later, the Newfie was sprawled out with his head on her lap. "You're such a goofball," she said, rubbing Captain's head.

"I'm sure the Chief is already looking into the will," I said, stifling another yawn. "Did you know your student was going to be there tonight?"

"Jessie? No, I was very surprised to see her," Missy said.

"So, she's taken some classes from you?" I said.

"Nothing gets past you," Josie said, laughing.

I made a face at her as I took a sip of coffee.

"She's taken a couple of my courses," Missy said. "She's a very good student. But I had no idea she'd also taken some from Bill."

"He's her *favorite* professor," Josie said, glancing at Missy. "Does that mean what I think it might?"

"That would be my initial assumption," Missy said, shrugging. "I'm afraid Bill shares some of the same tendencies that my ex-husband had."

"What on earth does she see in him? He's so pompous," I said.

"Jessie is young and impressionable," Missy said, shrugging. "I imagine she sees Bill as mature, even worldly. Give her a few months, she'll figure him out."

"And he was so mean to Jill's mom. I can't believe she only threw her champagne at him. I probably would have punched his lights out."

"Roger and Jennifer's fights were legendary," Missy said, finding some distant memory quite funny. "I was surprised to even see them sitting at the same table. Talk about mutual hatred."

"What I can't figure out is why Faith would want to kill Roger," I said.

"She's young and impressionable," Josie said. "Maybe she finally figured him out."

"That's no reason to kill him," I said.

"Well, she's obviously not the brightest crayon in the box," Josie said.

"No, you're right about that," Missy said. "When she was young, Bill was always saying that Faith's elevator didn't go all the way to the top floor. And he was sure she got that from her mother."

"That's cruel," I said, frowning. "I can't believe he said that about his own daughter."

"But that doesn't mean it's not accurate," Josie said. "And you've seen her temper in action."

"I guess," I said, frowning. "Still, there's something about this whole thing with Faith that's bothering me."

"Don't look at me," Josie deadpanned. "I did my part. I hit her as hard as I could."

Everyone laughed, and the dogs in front of the fire raised their heads in unison, took a quick look around the room, then went back to sleep.

"Did I happen to see you with Jackson tonight?" Chef Claire said, grinning at Missy.

"Oh, you caught that?" Missy said, blushing. "We just went for a little walk in the garden. He's a very nice man."

"He certainly is," Chef Claire said. "But be careful, he tends to bond pretty quickly."

"Yes, I picked up on that," Missy said. "He said he used to be the chief of police here."

"He was," Josie said. "But he and the town council had a parting of the ways, and Jackson decided to take over his parent's grocery store."

"He chose well," Missy said, shaking her head. "I can't imagine being a cop. Jackson invited me out on his boat tomorrow."

"So, you've decided to stick around for a few days?" I said.

"If you don't think it's too much of an imposition on you," Missy said. "I mean, I do have three dogs."

"Around here, three dogs is a rounding error," Josie said.

"Absolutely," I said. "Stay as long as you want. Maybe we'll get some answers to Roger's murder before you go."

"I suppose it should interest me more," she said, shrugging. "You know, the identity of the murderer. But it doesn't."

"Really?" I said, frowning at her. "You really don't care who killed him?"

"No," she said, shaking her head. "Not since I learned who all the suspects are. I can't stand any of them. It wouldn't break my heart regardless of who the killer turns out to be. And if it's Faith, so much the better. I guess that sounds pretty harsh, right?"

"Well, yeah. It kinda does, Missy," I said, staring at her.

Missy shrugged.

"There's just way too much history with those people," she said. "And as Bill always likes to say, the way to avoid repeating history is to understand what you're dealing with, learn what you can from it, and then move on."

"That's pretty good advice," Josie said. "Especially from a history professor."

"Oh, Bill is full of good advice," Missy said, grinning at Josie. "And I'm sure he'd be more than happy to give you all the private lessons you want."

"Thanks, but I think I'll pass," Josie said, scowling at the suggestion.

"He's always been the brightest crayon in the box," Missy said, still teasing Josie with the idea.

"I'm usually attracted to smart," Josie said, shaking her head. "But, no."

"His elevator definitely goes all the way to the top floor."

"Good for Bill," Josie said. "But after talking with him earlier, I'm afraid of what I might find in the basement."

Chapter 12

Unfortunately for him and his students, Bill wouldn't be giving anybody lessons, private or otherwise. I learned this stark fact early the next morning when my mother called me in a panic, her voice alternating between hysterical shrieks and hushed whispers tinged with despair. At first, I naturally assumed something was wrong with her, and I squeezed my coffee mug tight until she managed to convince me that she was fine. However, Bill's condition was apparently another matter altogether. Short on specifics and with my neurons on fire, I hung up and looked around the kitchen island where Josie, Chef Claire, and Missy were making short work of their stacks of French toast topped with maple butter and fresh strawberries.

"What's going on with your Mom?" Josie said, drizzling a generous portion of maple syrup over her second helping.

"Uh, she needs a bit of help," I said. "I told her I'd come over and give her a hand with the cleanup."

"Okay," Josie said, giving me a look that told me she knew I was lying through my teeth. But she said nothing. "I'd join you, but my morning is packed."

"I need to get to the restaurant to deal with a bunch of deliveries, but I could probably swing by her place in a couple of hours," Chef Claire said.

"No, don't worry about it, I'm sure the place was immaculate before she let the caterers leave. She probably just wants a second opinion on a few things," I said. "I'll be back as soon as I can."

I grabbed my keys, said a quick goodbye to all the dogs, then headed for my mom's house. I noticed the Chief's car in her driveway along with an unmarked state police cruiser. Just as I was getting out of my car, Freddie pulled in behind me. He hopped out, grabbed his bag from the back seat, and tossed it over his shoulder.

"We really need to stop meeting like this," he deadpanned.

"Tell me about it," I said, shaking my head. "My mother said something happened to Jill's dad."

We started to make our way up the driveway toward my mother's back door.

"Yeah, apparently, he's *history*," Freddie said. "Get it?"

"Geez, Freddie," I said, shaking my head at him. "How about you show a little respect for the guy?"

"First of all, if you spent all your time doing my job, your sense of humor would turn a little morbid, too. Second, I really don't think old Bill is gonna care one way or the other what sort of jokes I'm making."

"And you wonder why you're having such a hard time finding a girlfriend," I said, starting to huff and puff as I climbed the small incline.

We walked the rest of the way in silence, and my mother waved to us from her back porch. She walked down the steps, gave me a hug, then led us behind the house. The large tent was gone, and the lawn was immaculate. I lumbered way behind my mother's brisk pace but eventually made my way down the stone path that led to her large garden filled with plants and spring flowers. The main path intersected with several other smaller ones that were separated by manicured hedges about four feet tall. Every time I walked through the garden I was drawn back to my childhood where my friends and I spent countless hours playing hide and seek or tag. Later on, after I entered high school, my visits to the garden were usually reserved for those times when my boyfriend of the moment and I would sneak off for some alone time where I'd inevitably spend most of my time trying to teach him the finer points of keep away. But given the state of my love life, every time I walked the garden these days I was pretty much relegated to admiring the plants and flowers.

I stopped at a spot where two stone paths converged, and I glanced around for signs of my mother and Freddie. Not seeing either of them, I whistled softly.

"We're over here, darling."

I followed my mother's voice and was soon standing in a section of the garden I was very familiar with. Two wooden benches surrounded a birdbath, and two blue jays were enjoying a morning dip and ignoring the activity that surrounded them. Chief Abrams was talking to a state police detective next to Bill's body that was sprawled out on the ground in front of one of the benches. Freddie was already bent down and examining the body. I approached my mother and gave her another long hug, then waved at Chief Abrams. He and the detective strolled over.

"Good morning," Chief Abrams said.

"Hey, Chief," I said. "Hi, Detective Williams."

"Hi, Suzy," the detective said, then he noticed my quizzical expression. "Yeah, he's dead."

"Any signs of a struggle? Or wounds to the body?" I said, glancing back and forth at the two cops.

"No," Chief Abrams said.

"So, it's similar to what we saw with Roger in the restaurant?" I said, sneaking a quick peek at the body.

"So far," Detective Williams said. "I'd have to say it's almost identical."

"That means the same person killed both of them?" I said, grimacing as my temples started to pound.

"That's our guess," the Chief said. "But we can't be sure until we get some test results back." He glanced over at Freddie who was still hunched down over the body. "What do you think, Freddie? Since it's the second one with what looks like the same method, do you think we can get priority on the toxicology?"

"I can try, Chief," Freddie said, getting to his feet.

"I'll make a few calls," Detective Williams said.

"If the same person killed both of them, that shoots my theory out of the water," Chief Abrams said.

"How so?" I said.

"I really liked the daughter for the first one," the Chief said. "But if she did both of them, that would mean she was getting way too friendly with her own father. If you get my drift."

"Got it," I said, frowning. "That's disgusting, Chief."

"Yes, it is," he said. "And that's why I said it blows my theory out of the water."

"Not if Faith had the poison in a piece of candy or something like that," I said. "You know, they went for a little father-daughter walk in the garden, and she offered him something like a...oh, what's that candy called?"

"Are you talking about jelly candy?" Detective Williams said. "Like Spearmint Leaves or Orange Slices?"

"No, that's not it," I said, shaking my head.

"Chuckles?" the Chief said.

"That's it," I said, nodding.

"I loved those when I was a kid," Chief Abrams said. "Do they still make them?"

"Chuckles?" Detective Williams said. "I'm sure they do." He thought quietly for a moment. "Yeah, I guess that's possible."

"And she was walking around with that bag in her purse," I said. "Freddie, how long before you get the results back on the pills?"

"Who do I look like, Houdini?" Freddie said, scowling at us. "One of Detective Williams' guys is driving down this morning to drop it off at the lab. We might hear something tomorrow."

"That works," the Chief said.

"I just have one small question for you," Freddie said. "What possible motive would Faith have to kill her father?"

"I have no idea," the Chief said, shaking his head.

"That's why I still like the mother for it," Detective Williams said. "If she was capable of killing her current lover, I doubt if she'd think twice about getting rid of her ex-husband. Who, based on everything you've told me, she hated with a passion."

"I guess I can see that," I said, frowning.

"What's the matter?" the Chief said, staring at me.

"It's just too weird," I said. "We were just about to focus on Bill as a possible suspect in Roger's murder, then he shows up dead. Faith shows up at our table last night and drops a bag of suspicious looking pills on the table. And judging by the look on her face, she didn't have a clue what they were or what they were doing in her purse. Not to mention the two aunts who were pounding Kamikaze's all night. They had a history with Roger as well, and they both seem delighted that the guy was dead. And, of course, now we've got the mysterious woman who works for the catering company."

"What mysterious woman?" Detective Williams said, raising an eyebrow at me.

I spent a few minutes bringing him up to speed on the woman named Jessie. When I finished, Detective Williams jotted down a few notes. "I definitely want to talk with her."

"That shouldn't be a problem," I said. "She's spending the summer here working for her uncle."

"Good," the detective said, sitting down on one of the benches and rubbing his forehead. "Even if we get a match on the poison, you do know we could end up just chasing our tail on this one."

"I do," the Chief said, sitting down on the opposite bench. "Unless we get lucky and have a witness come forward. Even Faith can make a pretty good case for herself. When she went to the emergency room yesterday, she was separated from her purse for at least a couple of hours. Anybody could have put those pills in her bag. I don't know. I guess I still like her for both murders."

I felt my neurons surge, and I stared off into the distance. I closed my eyes and then began to slowly nod my head.

"Uh-oh," the Chief said, a grin starting to form. "She's got that look."

"Darling?"

"Yes, Mom?"

"Are you okay?"

"I'm fine."

"Darling, I've seen fine before. That isn't it."

"No, really," I said, blinking as I refocused on the others. "I'm okay."

"Talk to me, Suzy," the Chief said.

"It looks like we have somebody around who definitely wanted Roger and Bill dead, right?"

"Nothing gets past you," my mother said, laughing.

"Shut it, Mom," I said, making a face at her. "And right now, that person is probably walking around very confident, maybe even convinced, that they have gotten away with it."

"I think we're going to need a bit more, Suzy," the Chief said, glancing at the detective who was staring up at me, baffled.

"What if Bill really isn't dead?" I said softly.

"Uh, Suzy," Freddie said. "I've been doing this stuff quite a while, and I have to tell you in no uncertain terms that the guy laying at my feet is most definitely dead."

"Have you called it in yet?" I said, glancing back and forth at the Chief and the detective. "I mean, have you put it out on the radio that he's dead?"

"No," Detective Williams said. "The only thing that came over the radio was that assistance was needed here at your mom's place."

"After your mom called me, I only called Freddie and the state police," the Chief said. "And when I got here, it was pretty clear he was a goner, so I decided to wait to call an ambulance until Freddie had a chance to do his thing."

"Freddie, does anybody know you're here?" I said.

"Nope," he said, shaking his head.

"Mom, did you speak to anyone else?"

"No, darling," she said, frowning. "Is there a point to all these annoying questions?"

"Well, since we really don't have any solid clues about who did kill them, maybe we should try smoking the killer out," I said.

"And how do you suggest we do that?" Detective Williams said.

"By casually getting the word out that Bill isn't dead," I said, glancing around to gauge everyone's reaction.

"You want to fake the guy's death?" Freddie said, frowning.

"Actually, I think we'd be faking his *life*," I said with a small shrug.

"That's the goofiest thing I've ever heard," Detective Williams said.

"We really need to find you a boyfriend, darling. Have you completely lost your mind?"

"Anything's possible, Mom," I said, flashing her a quick smile before refocusing. "We could create a cover story about how Bill is in some sort of coma and has been admitted into intensive care at Upstate Medical. Do you think you could get the hospital administrators down there to go along with some sort of story like that?"

"If it was presented to them as a way to catch a murderer, they might," Detective Williams said, leaning forward on the bench. "But not if there was any chance we might be turning a killer loose in their hospital."

"That shouldn't be a problem," I said. "Obviously, Bill won't actually be there. And we could get the word out that there was a strict no-visitor policy in effect. Even if the mother or daughter showed up, they wouldn't be able to get in the room to see him." I focused on Detective Williams. "What do you think so far?"

"I'm gonna stick with goofy for the moment."

My mother and Chief Abrams snorted. I gave them a cold stare, then continued.

"After a day or two, we could get the word out that Bill was out of intensive care and being transferred back to the Clay Bay hospital."

"As well as let everybody know that his condition was still touch and go, but he was expected to eventually make a full recovery," the Chief said, nodding.

"Exactly," I said, beaming at him.

"And you're expecting that whoever killed him, just might show up at the hospital to finish the job?" Detective Williams said.

"Wouldn't you?" I said. "If there was a chance the person you thought you'd killed might make a full recovery and be more than happy to identify you to the police?"

"Yeah, I probably would at that," the detective said, nodding. "But I don't know, Suzy. I'm not even sure if this sort of thing would be legal."

"The guy's already dead," I said, shrugging. "It's not like we're putting him in any jeopardy. You can just send him on his way to the morgue with instructions for the people working there to keep their mouths shut for a couple of days."

"Still, I don't know," Detective Williams said, then he turned to Chief Abrams. "What do you think?"

"I don't like the idea of lying to the guy's family," the Chief said. "There's obviously no affection between any of them, but still…Nah, I don't like it."

"I don't like lying to them, either," I said. "But since the mom and daughter are two of the prime suspects, we obviously wouldn't be able to tell them." Then a neuron flared, and I flinched. "Jill. We need to call Jill."

"That'll ruin her honeymoon," my mother said.

"Yeah, it sure will. But as soon as the dust settles with her dad, they can head back down to Grand Cayman," I said.

"Will they be able to get away from work again?" my mother said.

"We'll make it work," I said.

"That's my girl," my mother said, patting my forearm. "But as far as your latest dose of insanity goes, I'm with the Chief. I don't like it."

"All I see in my future are all sorts of malpractice lawsuits," the Chief said, shaking his head.

"Tell me about it," Detective Williams said. "And there's no way I can run the risk of ending up in the same place with some of the creatures I've put away."

"Relax. You guys worry too much. I'm sure you'd get probation. Or a cushy stint at a country club prison at worst," I deadpanned.

But my attempt at humor was met with blank stares, so I decided to shift gears.

"We're trying to catch a murderer here," I said. "And who says she's going to stop at two? Maybe she has a whole list of people she plans to take out."

"You're convinced the killer's a woman?" Freddie said.

"I am. And as soon as she hears that Bill isn't dead, I'm betting there's a good chance panic is going to set in."

"Geez, I don't know, Suzy," the Chief said, shaking his head. "Pushing the envelope is one thing, but this is just-"

"Goofy," Detective Williams interjected.

"Aren't you forgetting something?" Freddie said.

"What's that?" I said.

"How would it be possible for somebody to survive cyanide poisoning?"

"Based on the guy laying on the ground, obviously it would appear to be impossible. I'll concede the point," I said. "But the killer doesn't know that. Maybe he only got a trace of the poison before he spit it out. Maybe it was a bad batch of cyanide or way past its expiration date."

"I don't think cyanide has an expiration date, Suzy," Freddie said.

"Geez, Freddie, I'm just spitballing here," I said, my voice rising. "Work with me."

"Getting back to goofy," Detective Williams said. "How exactly do you see this playing out?"

"Well, like I said, I'm still working my way through it," I said, turning defensive. "But if we can get the word out that Bill isn't being guarded when he comes back to the local hospital, the killer just might be lured back to finish the job. You know, slip in during the middle of the night, and take care of it. You've been in the hospital at night. It's very quiet, and we can work with the staff to make sure they make themselves scarce."

"And we'd be waiting in the hospital room for the killer to show up?" the Chief said.

"Sure," I said, nodding. "We'll just leave the lights off, and you'd be able to hide in there. But we'd need someone actually in the bed to make it realistic."

"That won't be a problem," the Chief said.

"You got somebody in mind?" Detective Williams said.

"Yeah. Me."

"What?" Chief Abrams said, staring in disbelief at me.

"Now hang on a second," my mother said. "You may have just crossed the line into clinically insane, darling, but you're still my daughter. I'm not comfortable letting you put yourself in that sort of danger."

"I'll be fine, Mom. The Chief and Detective Williams will be there the whole time."

"And it might be the only way we'll be able to keep a close eye on her and make sure she stays out of trouble," Chief Abrams said with a shrug.

"Well, there is that," my mother said, nodding. "But I really don't like the idea at all."

"Don't you want to stop a possible serial killer from doing it again?" I said.

"Not as much as I want a healthy daughter capable of giving me grandchildren," she said with a wistful stare into the distance. "Dare I dream."

"Don't start, Mom."

"I'm going to need to run this way up the chain of command," Detective Williams said.

"What do you think their reaction is going to be?" the Chief said.

"About covering up a murder and using a civilian guinea pig to try to catch the killer? What do you think their reaction is going to be?"

"I'm not sure I appreciate the guinea pig reference," I said, scowling at Detective Williams.

"Oh, I'm sorry. What term would you prefer? Lab rat? Bait?" he said, returning my stare.

"There's no need to get snarky, Detective," I said, pouting. "Guinea pig just has a lot of negative connotations. And now that I think about it, lab rat isn't much better."

"I'm not sure you can pull this off," the Chief said, chuckling. "You'd need to stay very still and keep your mouth shut at all times."

"Good luck with that," my mother said, laughing.

"You're a big help," I said, glaring at her.

"I can't believe you people are seriously considering doing this," Freddie said.

"Me either," the Chief and Detective Williams said in unison.

Chapter 13

Josie and Chef Claire popped bite-sized Snickers and listened closely with blank stares as I outlined my plan. My mother, having already heard the story, as well as run out of questions and the energy to protest any further, rested her head on the back of the couch in my office and closed her eyes. I finished, sat back in my chair, and put my feet up on the desk pleased with my performance.

"So, what do you think?" I said, glancing back and forth at them.

"I'm thinking about taking up base jumping," Josie said to Chef Claire.

"Good for you," Chef Claire said, nodding. "I'm planning on going on an African safari. I think a stuffed elephant head would look great over the fireplace."

"What?" I said, baffled.

"Oh, I thought we were playing *Who can up with the most insane idea?*" Josie said, shaking her head at me. "You know, that game you always win."

"You could at least try to be supportive," I said, pouting.

"Oh, I'm going to be supportive, Suzy," she whispered. "Rest assured, I'm going to do everything I can to make sure you get the best shrink money can buy."

Chef Claire and my mother both snorted.

"Funny. I think it's a great plan."

"I just have one question," Josie said.

"What?"

"Are you out of your freaking mind?" Josie said.

"Rhetorical, right?" Chef Claire said, grinning at her.

"Don't waste your breath, ladies," my mother said. "I've already gone ten rounds with her."

"I can't believe the cops are going along with it," Chef Claire said.

"Actually, they're still talking it over," I said. "They're a bit...*unsure* at the moment."

My mother snorted again.

"That's a very annoying habit, Mom."

"Is faking the guy's death even legal?" Chef Claire said.

"We're not faking his death," I snapped. "We're faking his life."

"Well, sure," Josie said. "Since you put it that way, that changes everything."

"Why do I even bother?" I said, removing my feet from the desk and sitting upright in my chair.

"Suzy," Josie said, turning philosophical. "I'll be the first person to admit, from time to time in the past, I've had some problems with some of your more outrageous ideas. Should I take a few moments to recount some of my personal favorites?"

"That won't be necessary," I said through clenched teeth.

"And when I have had problems with your theories or subsequent actions, I've always tried my best to discuss my concerns with you in a calm, measured fashion."

"Calm and measured? I must have dozed off during that part of the conversation," I said, glaring at her.

"We can sit here and debate that point all day, but, nonetheless, I feel the need to ask you a very important question," Josie said.

"You can lose the tone and attitude, Josie. I'm not a three-year-old."

"Current evidence to the contrary, I will concede the point," Josie said.

Chef Claire and my mother snorted again. I bit my bottom lip and waited for the surge of anger to pass.

"What's your question?" I said, taking a few deep breaths.

"At the risk of repeating myself," Josie said, leaning forward. "Are you out of your freaking mind?"

"I think it's the work of a genius," I said, transitioning into a full-on pout. "It's a brilliant plan."

"Laying in a hospital bed and waiting for a psychopath to shove a cyanide capsule down your throat with her tongue?"

"Yes."

Josie glanced back and forth at my mother and Chef Claire.

"Einstein would be so proud," Chef Claire said.

"Snoopmeister equals idiot times energy expended squared?" Josie said.

"Yeah, but I'm not sure I could do the math," Chef Claire deadpanned.

"I just don't understand why everyone is being so negative about this. And if it doesn't work, no harm, no foul, right?"

"Apart from the fact that you'll be lying to Jill's family," my mother said.

"Mom, for the tenth time, the guy is already dead," I said, then my voice trailed off to a whisper. "They just won't know that for a few days."

"Did you speak with Jill yet?" Josie said.

"Yeah, they're on their way back," I said.

"Did you tell her the truth?" Josie said.

"Of course," I said. "I told her everything."

"So, she knows her father is dead?" my mother said.

"Yes."

"And you told her about your plan to catch the killer?" Josie said.

"I did."

"And?"

"She thinks I'm nuts, too," I said, shrugging. "But she finally agreed to go along with it."

"That poor girl," my mother said.

"They weren't close at all," I said. "But it's still really tough to lose your dad."

"Yes, it is," my mother said. "But my sympathy was in reference to the fact that she has to work for you."

"Mom, would you please stop?" I snapped. "I'm way out on a limb as it is."

"Yes, young lady, you certainly are," she said, her voice rising. "And apparently determined to saw the limb off while you're still sitting on it."

I'd gotten the dreaded *young lady* out of her. It was time to change directions.

"Mom, I was wondering if I could borrow your pontoon boat," I said.

"You want to borrow the pontoon boat?" she said, confused. "Are you planning a party?"

"I thought it might be a good time to take all the women out for a nice relaxing day on the River."

"Here we go," Josie said, shaking her head.

"I can't wait to hear this," Chef Claire said.

"Since all of the women are sticking around for a few days, I thought it would be a nice idea if we invited them to spend the day cruising around. You know, to help them take their minds off the recent tragedies. We can pack a nice lunch, have a few drinks, take the dogs along for a swim."

"And get all the suspects in one place just to make sure they all hear the same version of whatever cover story you decide to use, right?" my mother said.

"You know me so well," I said, forcing a smile at her.

"Why am I seeing a whole bunch of lawsuits flashing before my eyes?" my mother said, staring up at the ceiling.

"Nobody is going to get sued, Mom," I said, doing my best to sound positive. But I made a mental note to check and make sure my personal liability policy was current. "Just remember we're trying to catch a murderer who has already killed two people."

"And your idea is to go out on the River with the killer and a bunch of potential additional victims?" Josie said.

"Nobody is going to get killed on the boat," I said, frowning. "We'll just be planting a few seeds." I glanced around at all three of them. "So, who's in?"

"Oh, count me in," Josie said, nodding. "This I gotta see."

"I'm in," Chef Claire said. "This is one of those stories I'm going to want to tell my grandchildren."

"Oh, how I wish that were possible," my mother whispered.

"Don't start, Mom, okay? Not today," I said. "Would you like to join us?"

"A day on the River with the Cyanide Killer?" my mother said. "Who could refuse an offer like that?"

Chapter 14

Sammy and Jill arrived home early the next afternoon, worn out, worried, and wondering aloud what the heck might happen next. Josie and I met them at C's for lunch, and the hostess escorted us to my mother's private table in a secluded corner of the dining room. Jill's eyes were red and puffy, and Sammy watched her closely, obviously concerned by how much pain his new bride was in.

"I'm so sorry, Jill," I said, squeezing her hand in support.

"Yeah, I can't imagine what you're going through," Josie said. "Not much of a honeymoon, huh?"

"They don't get much shorter," Sammy said, forcing a sad smile. "But we did get a chance to take a look around the airport and get a whiff of what we think was the ocean."

"Well, don't worry," I said. "We're going to fix that just as soon as we can. And when you head back to Cayman, you'll be going on a charter. My treat."

"And you'll be extending the honeymoon to two weeks," Josie said. "Not that it makes much difference at the moment given everything you're dealing with."

Sammy and Jill glanced at each other. Jill grabbed his hand and continued to grip it tight on top of the table.

"So, let me see if I've got this straight," Sammy said, frowning. "Jill's dad is dead, but you're telling everybody that he's in a coma and has a good chance of making a full recovery?"

"Yes," I said, nodding.

"And you're convinced that the killer is going to come back and try to finish the job?" he said, slowly talking his way through his thoughts.

"Yes, we are," I said.

Josie snorted.

"Okay," I said. "*I'm* convinced. Josie is still on the fence."

"Oh, I'm not even close to the fence," Josie said, picking up a menu and studying it. "I'm standing in a beautiful meadow miles away." She glanced up. "That's on the logic and reason side of the fence in case you were wondering."

"I think I agree with Josie," Sammy said. "Your plan sounds kind of-"

"Goofy," Josie said, refocusing on the menu. "Personally, I prefer clinically insane, but I got outvoted."

"Shut it."

"My dad was poisoned the same way that Roger was?" Jill said, frowning across the table at me.

"That's what it looks like," I said. "We should get some lab results back soon."

"It has to be Faith," Jill said, nervously drumming the fingers of her free hand on the table. "She hated our dad." She exhaled loudly. "But it's not like I was very fond of him, either."

"But why would she do that now?" I said. "It doesn't make any sense."

"Instead of trying to think her way through problems, Faith goes through life reacting. It's like she never learned that it's possible for human beings to insert the ability to choose in between a stimulus and her response. You saw her in action at the wedding."

"Did you hear anything specific from her or your dad on your wedding day?" I said.

"No, just the usual stuff," Jill said, shaking her head. "Faith was whining about how nobody understood everything she was going through. The problems she's always had to deal with. Blah, blah, blah, woe is me. She's such a narcissist. And then my dad started going off at one point about what a pain my mom was. Then he got all maudlin about how short life was and how important it was to make the right choices. But I figured that was just the booze talking."

"What sort of choices was he referring to?" I said, leaning forward.

"I'm sure he was talking about women," Jill said. "Apart from history, they were the only thing in life he ever had any real interest in exploring."

"He and I were talking at the reception, and he started bragging about some young student he was hooking up with," Sammy said, frowning. "He got pretty specific. I was really uncomfortable having that sort of conversation with my father-in-law, but it didn't seem to bother him at all."

"Was he talking about the woman who was working at the reception?" I said.

Sammy and Jill glanced at each other, then stared at me.

"What on earth are you talking about?" Jill said.

I took a few minutes to explain what we knew about Jessie, the woman who worked for the catering company. Soon, it became clear they didn't have a clue what or who I was talking about.

"My father managed to get his girlfriend, one of his students, assigned to work our reception?"

"No, we think it was a total coincidence," I said. "But we'll confirm it with her tomorrow on the boat."

"You invited her?" Jill said.

"Yeah, just in case it turns out she's somehow involved," I said, shrugging. "It's a total stretch, but it can't hurt, right?"

"I guess," Jill said, rubbing her forehead. "So, there's a good chance I'm going to be spending the day on the River with my father's killer?"

"Yes, I think it's almost a certainty," I said, finally picking up my menu.

"I'm not comfortable with that idea at all, Suzy," Sammy said. "How do you know the killer isn't going to try again tomorrow on the boat?"

"It doesn't fit the pattern," I said, shaking my head. "Whoever killed Roger and Jill's dad was very cautious about not getting caught."

"Apart from the fact that you heard her in the men's bathroom with Roger?" Josie said. "That doesn't sound very cautious to me."

"That was a calculated risk," I said, waving it off. "No, we're dealing with someone who is trying to fly way under the radar and probably plans on getting back to her former life just as soon as the dust settles."

My neurons flared, and I flinched.

"Are you okay?" Jill said, closely studying my expression.

I lowered my head and rubbed my temples. Josie reached into her bag and tossed a bottle of Advil across the table.

"Thanks," I said, swallowing three with a sip of water.

"Don't mind her," Josie said, tossing the bottle back into her bag. "Just give her a minute."

"Migraine?" Sammy said.

"No, neuron overload," I said, grimacing. Then I blinked and focused on Jill. "Your two aunts."

"What about them?"

"Were they around much when you were a kid?"

"Sure, until my parents got divorced. Up until then, both families lived close to each other and were very tight, But after the divorce, it was like everybody had to choose sides. When my mom decided to move, some folks on both sides of the family also decided to get out of New Hampshire."

"And your two aunts didn't spend much time in New Hampshire after that?"

"No, I don't think so," Jill said. "They both hated my dad, and I think their affairs with Roger were over. No, wait. That's not right. My Aunt Charlotte's affair with Roger didn't start until long after the divorce."

"Which one is she again?" Josie said, dredging a piece of Italian bread in olive oil.

"My mom's sister," Jill said. "You think she might be involved in this?"

"Not necessarily," I said, rubbing my forehead. "I need to eat something." I grabbed a piece of bread and dipped it in the oil. I chewed slowly and tried to force my thoughts down a coherent path. "I'm just trying to sort out the timelines so we might be able to eliminate some of the potential suspects."

"Who *have* you been able to eliminate?" Sammy said.

"Well, there's you and Jill," I said, dipping another piece of bread in the olive oil.

"It's a start," Josie said, laughing. "And there's you, your mom, and me and Chef Claire."

"The jury is still out on you," I said.

"Funny," she said, making a face at me. "I wasn't even thinking about the Kamikaze Kids. That is an interesting thought, Snoopmeister."

"Did you know that your Aunt Charlotte and your dad also had something going on between them?" I said to Jill.

"Where did you hear that?"

"Your Aunt Trudy mentioned it between Kamikazes," I said.

"I never heard about it," she said, shaking her head. "But I wouldn't put it past either one of them."

"Your family is like a bunch of rabbits," Josie said, glancing over at Jill. "No offense."

"None taken," Jill said. "That was just one more reason on a long list why I got as far away from them as soon as I could."

"Fluffle," I said softly, still trying to organize my thoughts.

"What?" Josie said, frowning at me.

"A group of rabbits is called a fluffle."

"It is?"

"Yeah."

"I did not know that," Josie said. "So, Jill's family members on both sides indiscriminately jumping into bed with each other is what's caused all this ker-fluffle?"

"Nice try. The word you're looking for is *kerfuffle*."

"Yeah, but mine's funnier."

"Don't start."

"Oh, it's way too late to be worrying about that," Josie said. "What time are we heading out tomorrow?"

"I told everyone to meet us at Rooster's at noon," I said. "Your schedule looked open in the afternoon. That reminds me. Would you mind helping out at the Inn tomorrow, Sammy? I know you're supposed to be on your honeymoon, and I hate asking."

"Not a problem. Compared with your day, being surrounded by dogs sounds pretty good."

"Thanks," I said, then turned to Josie. "You're okay with that, right?"

"I told Missy I'd take a look at her labs in the morning. She says they're due for their final round of vaccines. I also want to get them started on their heartworm regimen. And then I have a spaying scheduled at ten. But, yeah, noon works for me."

"I know it does," I said. "That's why I told everyone we were leaving at twelve."

"You are in a mood, aren't you?" Josie said.

"I'm just nervous," I said. "I'm not exactly sure what I've gotten myself into."

"Well, don't worry about it," Josie said, sitting back in her chair as our server approached. "If the guinea pig thing doesn't work out for you, I'm sure something else will turn up."

I stared at Josie, knowing she wasn't done. I sat back in my chair and waited.

"Crash test dummy comes to mind."

Chapter 15

It was overcast when the sun first began making its way above the horizon, but by mid-morning, the clouds had burned off, and it was one of those perfect spring days that was filled with the promise of summer. I'd been up since five, not because I was that much of an early-riser, but due to the fact that my neuron-induced headache had continued unabated since the previous day. But as I sat outside on the porch staring out at the water sipping coffee and enjoying the company of all seven dogs, my headache began to subside, and I was able to start organizing my thoughts for the day. I glanced down at Chloe and Captain who were both sound asleep on my feet and smiled at the idea that as long as both dogs could be in contact with even a tiny spot on their human companions, they felt content and safe. Missy's three labs were also sound asleep and tucked tight against Dente, Chef Claire's female Golden, whose maternal instincts had surfaced in a major way as soon as the three puppies had arrived. Al, the male Golden, was keeping a watchful on things as he groomed himself. He caught me watching him, got to his feet, and dropped his head in my lap. I stroked it gently as I pondered our upcoming day on the St. Lawrence.

My plan was to take the boat across the main channel, then spend most of the day drifting in the calm water of the Lake of the Isles. The water was still too cold for any normal person to swim in, but I knew the dogs would love it. Apart from getting drenched every time the dogs got out of the water and shook, I really wasn't worried about anything bad happening while we were out on the boat. In fact, although the killer would probably be in close proximity all day, I was very much looking forward to being out on the water. And despite the fact that my mother's party boat could finish fifth in a four-vessel race, it was incredibly comfortable, and we borrowed it every chance we got when we wanted to go out on the River with a group of friends and their dogs.

Or with a group of women that included someone who had already killed two people.

I got about halfway through my strategy before Chef Claire and Josie joined me on the porch carrying big coffee mugs. The dogs stirred as they sat down, changed places and positions, then settled back down to enjoy the rest of their morning nap.

"What time did you get up?" Josie said.

"Around five. It's beautiful out here."

"It is. Five, huh? Couldn't get the neurons to shut down?"

"No. They're on fire."

"Suzy, I really wish you'd reconsider this whole thing," Josie said.

"I'll be fine," I said, staring out at the water.

"Why don't you just let the Chief and the rest of the cops handle it?" Chef Claire said.

"That's rhetorical, right?" I said, grinning at her.

"Yeah. I forgot who I was talking to," Chef Claire said, sipping her coffee. "But promise us you'll be careful, okay?"

"We're just going out on the boat," I said, glancing back and forth at them.

"We're not talking about today," Josie said. "We're talking about tonight."

"Don't worry about it," I said, my voice breaking as it rose. "The Chief and Detective Williams will be in the room the whole time. Not to mention all the extra cops who'll be outside the hospital."

"Okay," Josie said, then glanced over at me. "You do know that you're probably going to have to wear one of those hospital gowns."

"What?" I said, frowning.

"Yeah, one of those open gowns that tie in the back," Josie deadpanned.

"No way," I said, shaking my head. "I'm not wearing one of those things."

"I don't know, Suzy," she said. "It's probably hospital policy."

"I know what you're trying to do, Josie."

"I'm just saying," she said, glancing at Chef Claire. "Those things are pretty revealing. And we all know how much you like showing your goods off."

"I'm not wearing one of those gowns," I said firmly. "I'll just keep the covers pulled up."

I glanced back and forth at Chef Claire and Josie who were enjoying the conversation way too much.

"I just hope for your sake you don't have to get out of bed," Josie said. "You should probably avoid drinking too many fluids.

The last thing you want is to have to get up and pee at the wrong moment."

"I'm sure the Chief and Detective Williams wouldn't mind," Chef Claire said.

"Just make sure you tie the gown really tight. Those things can be really drafty," Josie said.

"I think she'll look cute in a hospital gown," Chef Claire said. "Maybe she can accessorize it with a pair of those non-skid socks and a rolling IV pole."

"Sexy. I like it," Josie deadpanned. "She could pose by the window with her hair down, one hand on her hip, and a come hither look on her face."

"She'd be, what's the word…alluring?" Chef Claire said as she fought back laughter.

"I'm gonna go with irresistible," Josie said.

"You're really not funny," I said, glaring back and forth at them.

"Disagree," Josie said, finally breaking up. "What shade of lipstick are you thinking about wearing?"

"I'm going to go shower," I said, gently removing Al's head from my lap.

"Good idea," Josie said, calling after me. "You're probably only going to get sponge baths once you get admitted."

Chapter 16

We decided to use a mini-caravan for the short drive to Rooster's marina. Actually, marina is a bit of a stretch. It's more of a haphazard collection of boathouses and floating, interlocking wooden docks that contain boat slips of various sizes, a couple of gas pumps, a workshop where Rooster spends most of his time tinkering with small engines, and a tiny clapboard general store where he sells wildly overpriced sundries to unsuspecting tourists. Josie and Chef Claire both drove and split the seven dogs up between the two cars. Missy hopped into the passenger seat of my SUV, and we made the short drive to the apartment complex where Jessie, her student who worked for the catering company, was staying for the summer. She was already waiting for us on the sidewalk when I pulled in.

"Good morning," Jessie said, climbing into the back seat. "It's nice to see you again, Professor McNamara. And thanks so much for the invitation, Ms. Chandler. I can use a day on the River to take my mind off what happened to Bill. I have to say that I'm really worried."

I glanced through the rearview mirror and saw her wringing her hands as she stared out the window.

"Don't worry. I'm sure everything is going to work out just fine," Missy said, glancing over her shoulder.

"We're just glad you could make it, Jessie," I said, sneaking another peek at her through the mirror. "And nobody calls me Ms. Chandler."

"Got it," she said, giving me a friendly salute. "Suzy it is."

Interesting, I thought. I'd gotten the dreaded Ms. Chandler. She referred to Missy as Professor McNamara. But it was Bill for the recently deceased. But I guess if she had been sleeping with the guy, calling him Professor in the throes of passion might sound a little weird. Unless they'd been into some sort of strange teacher-student, role-playing thing. Or maybe Bill had just been on a first name basis with all his students.

I squinted through the windshield as my neurons flared, raising all sorts of random questions that threatened to send me scurrying off on several different tangents chasing wild geese. I rubbed my forehead as I flipped my turn signal on.

I needed to pace myself. I had a long day ahead of me.

I pulled into the gravel parking lot and climbed out of the car. Josie and Chef Claire were already there with the dogs, and Chloe made a mad dash for me as soon as she spotted me. I knelt down to pet her. She knew where we were going, and she began to gently tug at my sleeve to get a move on.

"Hold your horses," I said, laughing.

Rooster was chatting with Josie and Chef Claire, then he laughed loudly at something Josie said and glanced over at me. He shook his head in apparent disbelief then waved me over. Missy and Jessie strolled down to one of the docks and stared out at the River. I couldn't blame them for doing that. The view was spectacular.

"Good afternoon, Rooster," I said, giving him a hug. "What nonsense have these two been filling your head with?"

"Don't worry. It's nothing that your mother hasn't already told me."

"She told you?"

"Of course," Rooster said. "Your mother and I don't have any secrets. At least none that either one of us knows about." He laughed at his own joke and shook his head at me again. "You are something else."

"I'm going to take that as a compliment," I said.

"Take it however you want," he said, shrugging. "But I think you're nuts."

"Okay, I think we're done with this conversation. Is the boat ready?" I said, glancing at the nearest boathouse.

"It's all set," he said. "I'll back it out as soon as everybody gets here and park it next to pump one."

"Thanks," I said, then noticed the blank stare he was giving me. "What?"

"Why don't you let someone else handle the hospital bed? Like me."

"No, it was my idea, and it's something I need to do," I said, shaking my head.

"How about I just forbid you to do something that stupid?" he said, cocking his head at me.

"How about you just mind your own business?" I said, glaring at him.

"Whoa," Rooster said with a grin. "Somebody got up on the snarky side of the bed."

"I'm sorry, Rooster," I said, immediately chagrined about barking at my good friend. "It's just that these two got me wound up this morning."

"Now it's our fault," Josie said to Chef Claire.

"I thought we were very helpful," Chef Claire said, laughing.

I let it pass and turned around when I heard a car pull into the parking lot. Jill, along with her mother and Faith, got out of the car. It looked like none of them were speaking to each other, and Jill watched her mother and sister wander down to the docks, then headed our way. Josie nudged me, and I followed her eyes toward Faith who was tiptoeing her way across the gravel wearing open-toed pumps with what appeared to be four-inch heels.

"Stiletto heels on a boat?" Josie said, shaking her head.

"Let's make sure she takes them off before she boards," I said. "If she punches a hole in the deck or one of the leather cushions my mom will kill her."

"Works for me," Josie said, glancing over. "I'll even be her alibi."

"Just try to take it easy today, okay?" I said, then gave Jill a big hug. "Hey. Glad you could make it. How are you holding up?"

"I'm a bit better today."

"I'm glad to hear that," I said, giving her another hug. "Where are your aunts?"

"Your mom is picking them up," Jill said softly. "I was worried that Aunt Charlotte and my mom would start duking it out in the back seat."

"This is going to be so much fun," Josie said, glancing in Faith's direction. "What sort of mood is Beelzebub in today?"

"Dark and cloudy," Jill said. "I wouldn't stand too close to the edge of the boat if I were you. But at the moment, she's more worried about how she's going to handle being around the dogs all day."

"That's right," Josie said, snapping her fingers. "I forgot. She's afraid of dogs. That might come in handy."

"Please, don't start," I said, frowning at her. "Try to remember why we're here."

"I thought we were here to eat and drink," Josie said.

"I know that's why I'm here," Chef Claire said.

My mother arrived in her Range Rover, the most recent addition to her car collection, and she climbed down out of the vehicle and waved. She was wearing sunglasses and a fedora along with a color coordinated blouse and shorts ensemble that should have looked odd, but somehow worked perfectly. She had a light sweater draped over her shoulders and was wearing a pair of white, Christian Louboutin slip-on sneakers that probably cost more than my entire shoe collection. All of us stared at her as she approached.

"She kind of takes the worry out of getting old," Josie said, giving my mother an admiring look.

"She certainly does," I said, nodding.

"She looks fantastic," Chef Claire said.

"Good afternoon, all," my mother said. She gave all of us hugs and pecks on the cheek. Then she stood back and gave me the once-over. "Really, darling? Cutoff jeans? Where did I go wrong, Rooster?"

"They're comfortable," I said, protesting.

"So is being nestled in the arms of the right man, darling," she said, raising an eyebrow. "But I don't see you in any hurry to try that on for size."

"Geez, Mom. Can't you wait until we at least leave the dock?"

"You might want to go easy on her, Mrs. C.," Josie said. "She's a little nervous about her big date tonight."

Everyone laughed way too loud and long, and I shook my head as I headed for the boathouse.

"I assume the key is in the ignition," I said, glancing back at Rooster.

"It is," Rooster said, still chuckling.

I entered the boathouse and untied the lines. I climbed down into the pontoon boat and fired up the twin seventy-five horsepower outboard motors. I slowly backed the forty-foot craft out of the boathouse, turned it around, and soon came to a stop at the large dock that fronted Rooster's property. I shut the engines off, then hopped out and quickly tied the bow and stern to two cleats that were fastened into the dock.

"You've done this before," Jill's mother said, standing nearby on the dock and giving me a nod of approval.

"Way too many times to count," I said, smiling up at her.

"It's a very interesting boat," she said, glancing around at it. "I don't think I've ever seen anything quite like it."

"Rooster built it," I said. "My mom happened to mention that she would love to have a party boat, and this is what he surprised her with. Come on, climb aboard and I'll give you the nickel tour."

I helped her into the boat then remembered the major con job I was playing on her. She had just lost her estranged husband but didn't know it. She also didn't know that she was near the top of my list of suspects for two murders. My deceit made me feel small, but I focused on the bigger picture that I was sure was going to play out later tonight and regrouped.

"What are those things on the sides under the boat?" she said, glancing over the edge.

"The pontoons? Oh, they're airtight aluminum tubes that Rooster welded together," I said. "That's what makes it float."

"Interesting," she said. "It seems remarkably well-equipped for what would appear to be a rather makeshift craft."

"Well, there's not much that's makeshift about it. The deck is a high-end reinforced fiberglass, and all the railings are brass and mahogany. There's a folding canvas roof you can pull up if it starts to rain or you just want some shade. There are benches along the port and starboard side that pull out that can easily seat twenty-five people. The counter that runs across the stern is the bar and kitchen."

"You have a kitchen?" she said, surprised.

"You're new here, right?" I said, laughing.

"What?"

"Nothing," I said, shaking my head. "Yeah, the kitchen was a must have. It's got a stove and a mini-fridge. And a built-in cooler. It all runs on propane."

"Fascinating," she said, taking it all in. "And you say that your friend, Rooster, built all of this?"

"He did," I said, nodding. "In fact, he probably uses it more than any of us."

"He looks like a very interesting man," she said, glancing in his direction. "Will he be joining us today?"

"No, it's just us girls," I said.

I couldn't miss the look she was giving Rooster and immediately felt a bit better about lying to her. Apparently, my initial assumption of her being estranged and heartbroken missed the mark, and she was coming across as a woman on the prowl rather than a grieving divorcee with a dead boyfriend and an ex-husband lying in a coma. My neurons flared as the question of whether or not she was the one who killed Roger and Bill again began bouncing around in my head. I got as far as a definite maybe, then got stuck in a loop. I shook it off and continued the tour.

"The structure near the bow is the head," I said, pointing.

"Head means bathroom, right?" she said, frowning.

"It does," I said.

"It's not something I expected to see," she said, glancing around the exterior of the fiberglass structure.

"Trust me, after a couple of drinks and a few hours out on the River, you'll be very glad it's there."

We both glanced at the dock when we heard the sound of everyone making their way toward the boat. The dogs led the way, and our four expertly hopped into the boat and began exploring their options about where to sit. Missy's three labs were less experienced but nonetheless excited about the prospect of a boat ride. They stood at the edge of the dock wagging their tails furiously. I laughed at the sight, then gently lifted them one at a time and set them down on the deck. All seven dogs were soon clustered in the bow, obviously anxious to get started. My mother was chatting and laughing with Jill's aunts as they made their way onto the boat and sat down. Jill was chatting quietly with Jessie, and I extended a hand to help both of them climb aboard. I glanced back at the dock where Faith was slowly wobbling her way down the dock. Her bright red stiletto pumps were gorgeous but about as appropriate to wear on a boat as it was to use a tennis racket to go fishing. Josie and Chef Claire were walking behind her, each holding a handle on the large ice chest they were carrying between them.

I stared at Faith's shoes, then looked at Josie and Chef Claire who shrugged and shook their heads. Moments later, Faith came to an abrupt stop when one of her stilettos got wedged between two dock planks. She tried to free her leg, but the shoe wasn't going anywhere. She muttered and cursed under her breath, and her face was flushed red with anger and embarrassment. She noticed Josie staring at her predicament and glared at her.

"You got something you want to say?" Faith said.

"You don't spend a lot of time around boats, do you?" Josie said, kneeling down.

163

"It's never been high on my list of priorities," Faith snapped.

"And boaters everywhere thank you," Josie said, examining the situation. "You're going to have to take your shoe off."

Faith exhaled loudly then stepped out of the shoe. She hobbled around on one heel for a few seconds, then removed her other shoe. Josie tugged at the wedged shoe, then pulled harder. Josie grunted and jerked hard, and she fell backward onto the dock when the shoe finally came free. But Josie lost her grip, and the shoe floated through the air. Faith let out a shriek, dashed toward it, and snatched it out of mid-air. But her momentum carried her forward, and she teetered on the edge of the dock, frantically waved her arms to catch her balance, then toppled forward into the water with a loud splash. Everyone in the boat stared over the sides at her as she surfaced and gasped for air.

"This water is freezing," Faith gasped as she tried to find her bearings and catch her breath.

Captain, concerned with her safety, climbed up on top of the bow and jumped in. He landed right next to her and grabbed her sleeve and began to pull her toward shore. Faith, not convinced that rescuing her was what was on Captain's mind, screamed at the dog and tried to free her arm from his clutches. Captain misunderstood her movements and assumed she wanted to play. He barked loudly, then placed a paw on top of her head and dunked her. He continued to bark and swim in small circles around her.

"Get this creature away from me!" Faith cried out as she started to hyperventilate.

"Captain!" Josie said. "Come here. Come."

The Newfie reluctantly left his swim buddy and made his way to the steps that led back up to the dock. He shook violently, climbed back on the boat, then put his paws up on the side and stared down at Faith who was slowly paddling her way back to the dock. Everyone on the boat turned to look at Josie who was watching the scene play out with a big grin.

"Don't look at me," Josie said when she noticed our stares. "I didn't push her. She fell in."

"She *fell?*" I said, raising an eyebrow at her.

"Yeah, she did. As the result of an ill-fated, shoe-rescue mission."

Josie shrugged at us, then nodded at Chef Claire to lift her side of the ice chest. They carried it onto the boat, emptied the contents into the cooler and fridge, then sat down in the stern. Faith, shivering and looking like a drowned rat, climbed aboard and my mother handed her a towel and draped a blanket around her shoulders.

"Why don't you have a seat out in the sun, dear?" my mother said, consoling her. "You'll warm up in a few minutes."

"I hate this place," Faith said, loud enough for everyone to hear. Then she glared at Faith. "Why couldn't you have gotten married somewhere normal? Like Vegas."

"Maybe next time," Jill said, staring out at the water.

"Okay, let's get this show on the road," my mother said, sitting down behind the wheel.

The boat left the dock, and Rooster waved goodbye then headed back toward his workshop shaking his head. I knew exactly how he felt.

"Who's ready for a Kamikaze?" Chef Claire said, holding up a large plastic pitcher.

"You brought Kamikaze's?" Charlotte said, nudging Trudy who was sitting next to her.

"Only a gallon," Chef Claire said, laughing.

"Well, then I guess we'll just have to pace ourselves," Trudy said, accepting two glasses from Chef Claire.

"Speak for yourself," Charlotte said, draining half of her drink.

I sat down next to my mother and stretched my legs out.

"Beautiful day," I said, glancing over at her.

"It's not the day I'm worried about, darling."

Chapter 17

A half-hour later, we arrived at the entrance to the Lake of the Isles, and my mother put the boat in neutral then shut the engines down. The breeze was warm and light, and the water shimmered in the sun like a massive sheet of blue-green glass. Since it wasn't the weekend and still way too early in the season to avoid frostbite-free water skiing, we were the only boat around, and the silence was broken only by the sound of two loons chatting. The dogs cocked their heads at the noise, then Chloe glanced over at me with an expectant look on her face.

"Sure, go ahead," I said, grabbing a bag of tennis balls next to me.

"My babies have never been in the water before," Missy said, frowning. "Do you think they'll be okay?"

"Yeah, I like their chances," I said, tossing one of the balls into the water.

All four of our dogs dove off the bow and were soon in hot pursuit of the tennis ball that was bobbing about fifty feet from the boat. The three young labs were perched on the bow, desperate to join their buddies in the water, but not comfortable making the jump. Uncertain about how to get in the water, they padded back and forth barking at the other dogs. Josie headed for the bow, removed a small folding set of steps from underneath one of the benches and hooked it over the side of the boat. She gently lifted the black lab onto the top step, and the dog surveyed the situation then made his way down the remaining two steps into the water. Soon, he was swimming rapidly toward the other dogs.

"I think he likes it," Josie said, grinning back at us.

The other two labs headed for the steps and made their into the water with no help.

"Smart dogs," Josie said, nodding.

I fired several more tennis balls into the water, and a mad scramble for them ensued.

"Okay, I'll keep an eye on the dogs while you guys grab a bite to eat," I said, sitting down on the sundeck that stretched across the bow.

"You want me to bring you a plate?" Josie said.

"No, thanks. I'll eat in a bit."

Josie and Missy headed for the stern, and I watched the dogs paddle through the water and wrestle with each other. As always, Captain was a dominating presence, but all four of the adult dogs kept a close, protective eye on the labs. I continued to stare out at the water for a few minutes, then turned around when I felt the presence of someone standing behind me.

"They look like they're having a lot of fun," Jessie said.

"Yeah, they love coming over here," I said. "Come on up and have a seat."

Jessie climbed up next to me and stretched her legs over the edge. Her feet remained suspended about two feet above the water.

"So, this is how you spend your life?" Jessie said.

"This is certainly a big part of it," I said, nodding.

"Good life."

"Yeah, I've got nothing to complain about."

Finally, something I didn't need to lie about: The quality of my life was an unassailable truth, and it was probably about as perfect as anyone could ever expect. Apart from a scrambled-neuron headache that was making my temples pound.

"So, tell me a bit about yourself, Jessie."

"There's really not much to tell. I haven't done anything yet."

"Well, that's understandable. You're still pretty young. What are you, twenty?"

"I just turned nineteen," she said, laughing at Captain who now had three tennis balls in his mouth. "How does he get all of them in his mouth?"

"He gets that from his mother," I said, laughing. "And your Uncle Bobby owns the catering company?"

"No, Bobby's not my uncle," Jessie said, shaking her head.

"Oh, I heard he was your uncle," I said, frowning. "Friend of the family?"

"More like family of a friend," she said. "I don't have any family."

"I'm so sorry to hear that," I said, turning toward her. "You're an orphan?"

"Yeah," she whispered. "My parents died in a plane crash when I was six."

"That's awful," I said, as always feeling helpless about being unable to come up with anything better when trying to respond compassionately to tragic events.

"Yes, it certainly was. It was in all the papers," she said, staring out at the water. "Noted airplane designer and his wife die in a fiery accident."

"Really?" I said, frowning. "Where was this?"

"Somewhere over the Nevada desert," she said. "My father did a lot of work for the government, and that's where most of the protected airspace is. Or so I've been told."

"What happened?"

"He and my mom were doing a test flight with one of his new planes," Jessie said softly. "But he got some of the math wrong when he designed it, and the wings cracked then fell off at fifteen thousand feet."

I thought about my own intense fear of flying and shuddered.

"I don't know what to say," I said.

"What can you say?" she said with a shrug. "So, I spent the next twelve years as a ward of the state bouncing around foster homes. You have no idea how happy I was when I turned eighteen and got accepted into college."

"You just finished your freshman year?"

"I did," she said. "And when one of my roommates mentioned that her uncle had a catering company up here and

170

was looking for someone to help out this summer, I jumped on it."

"Who's your roommate?"

"Sandy Wilkins," Jessie said.

"Oh, I know Sandy. Bobby's her uncle?" I said, glancing over at her.

"I can never follow her family tree," Jessie said. "He might only be her cousin, but she calls him her uncle. It's very complicated."

"It is," I said, laughing. "The Wilkins' have a very big family. I've never been able to keep it all straight, either. I haven't seen Sandy around. What's she up to?"

"She's spending the summer backpacking through Europe with her boyfriend."

"Nice," I said, nodding. "So, you just decided to spend the summer here?"

"Yeah, I needed to get away from New Hampshire for a while, and Sandy is always talking about how beautiful it is up here. She wasn't lying."

"No, she wasn't," I said, glancing around the calm water as the soft breeze kicked up a notch. "Chloe. No."

Chloe had apparently had enough of Captain hogging all the tennis balls and was tugging hard on one of his ears.

"I said no," I called out, doing my best not to laugh. "She's such a beast." I refocused on Jessie. "You must have been surprised to see Bill and Missy at the wedding."

"I was shocked," she said. "But not nearly as shocked as I was when I heard what happened to Bill. I was devastated. I still am."

"I take it the two of you were close," I said, deciding to toss my line into the water to see if I got a nibble.

She didn't miss the inference, and she stared at me. Then she shrugged and smiled.

"Yeah, I've been sleeping with him," she said as a simple statement of fact. "That's some real breaking news. A young female student sleeping with one of her professors. I'm such a cliché, right?"

"Hey, I'm not judging. You're old enough to make your own decisions."

"One would think," she said softly.

"Aren't you interested in any of the guys your own age?"

"Drunken frat-rats and tech-heads?" she said, frowning. "Thanks, but I'll pass."

"Got it. I imagine Bill must have seemed very different from them," I said, then bit my bottom lip for the slip-up. "I mean he *is* different."

"Yeah, he is. I have some pretty basic requirements when it comes to men, and he meets most of them," she said. "Decent table manners, capable of having an intelligent conversation, and knowing their way around a wine list is a definite plus. And, of course, someone who's able to get my motor running if you catch my drift."

"Sure, sure," I said, staring out at the water. "So, do you think the two of you have a future together?"

"Oh, absolutely not," she said, scowling. "Bill is just one of those life experiences every girl is supposed to have, right?"

"I guess," I said. "But what do I know? I didn't have that particular experience in college."

"It's no big deal. Bill's just a little something for the memory bank. You know what I mean?"

"I am familiar with the memory bank," I said, massaging my temples.

"Truth be told, I'm just trying to make it through college in one piece."

"I see. And you think he can help?"

"Oh, he's definitely helping. I'm just not sure how long it's going to last," she said. "But if he doesn't make it out of his coma, I guess I'm not going to have to worry about that, huh?"

I flinched at the bluntness of her comment but said nothing.

"That sounded harsh, didn't it?" Jessie said.

"Well, maybe a little," I said, glancing over at her.

"I've just gotten used to losing people," she said. "People have always told me that going through a tragedy like that at an early age helps toughen you up for the other things in life that are going to happen. But instead of tough, I think it just made me hard and cold."

"You don't seem hard and cold, Jessie."

"You barely know me," she said, laughing. "Give it some time."

"At least you haven't lost your sense of humor," I said, laughing along. Then I made direct eye contact with her. "I want to ask you a question. But I should probably warn you that it might come across as a bit inappropriate."

"Go right ahead. I'm very used to people asking me inappropriate questions."

"Who do you think tried to murder Bill?"

She met my stare and thought about the question for several seconds. Then she rubbed the side of her face and looked away to gaze out at the water.

"It's a reasonable question. Based on what Bill's told me about both of them, it either has to be his deranged ex-wife or that narcissist posing as his daughter."

"Deranged?"

"Absolutely. If there's one thing I recognize, it's deranged," she said, glancing behind her toward the stern where Jennifer was in the middle of an animated conversation with her sister, Charlotte. "Look at her. Do you see the way she's waving her hands around? That's a classic sign of someone who isn't comfortable just using words to make her point. And she's getting very frustrated about not being able to get her message across. I'd say she's about ten seconds away from either punching her or getting up and walking away."

We continued to watch the conversation play out, then Jennifer made a final comment and walked away from her sister in a huff.

"Wow, you're good," I said, laughing. "Maybe you should forget about history and major in psychology."

"I'd rather die than study psychology," she said, shaking her head at Jennifer. "It's no wonder Bill slept around during their marriage."

"I thought she was the one who was sleeping around," I said, trying to remember what I'd been told.

"I imagine it was a mutual agreement," Jessie said. "But, who cares, right? At least they both got out in one piece."

"You seem to like that reference," I said, my neurons flaring.

"What? The one piece thing?"

"Yeah."

"Lately, I've been reading a lot about the importance of trying to live a complete life," she said, shrugging. "And the one piece metaphor really resonates with me. But what do I know? I'm nineteen."

"What are you two talking about?"

We both turned and saw Missy standing behind us staring out at the dogs who continued to do battle over the tennis balls.

"Hey, Professor McNamara. We were just talking about Bill and Jennifer," Jessie said. "You didn't miss anything important."

"I'm sure I didn't," Missy said, laughing. "How are my babies doing out there?"

"They're doing great. And I was just getting ready to herd them all back to the boat," I said, sliding off the bow. "They'd be happy to spend all day out there, but they've had enough for now. And in about five minutes, they'll all be sound asleep."

"How do you get them out of the water?" Missy said.

"Watch," I said, leaning over the edge of the boat facing the dogs. I whistled sharply once, and all seven dogs began treading water and staring up at me. "Let's go. Back to the boat."

Captain woofed his displeasure at me as he continued to paddle in place.

"Don't argue with me, Captain. I said, let's go."

Captain, joined by Chloe, barked again.

"Okay, so you want to play it that way, huh?" I held my hands about a foot apart, palms up. "Snack?" I said, then let the question hang in the air.

Captain and Chloe, followed by Al and Dente, made a beeline for the boat. The three young labs trailed behind paddling furiously.

"Rule number one," I said, laughing. "Always try to be smarter than your dogs. There are some towels under that bench over there. Grab a bunch of them. And you might want to head to the stern for a few minutes unless you feel like taking a very cold shower."

"Is it snack time?" Josie said as she approached.

"Yeah, I think they're starting to wear out," I said, tossing her one of the towels.

"Here comes the fun part," Chef Claire said, catching both towels I threw her.

Missy and Jessie took a few steps back as Josie headed for the steps hanging off the side of the boat. Captain led the way up, hopped up on the railing, then jumped down onto the deck and shook vigorously.

"Chance of showers, one hundred percent," Josie said, hunching over and shielding her head with her arms.

Chloe, then Al and Dente, repeated the same process. Josie helped the labs back into the boat. They stood on the deck and shook. I tossed Missy a towel, then a second as she dried her three dogs. When we finished, we wiped the deck with the used towels and spread them out on the sun deck to dry.

"That's quite a process you guys have worked out," Jessie said. "Good job."

"Thanks," I said, wiping my hands on my shorts. "It took us a while, but we finally figured out a way to stay reasonably dry."

Chef Claire handed us small plastic bags that contained her latest creation.

"What is this?" Missy said, staring at the bag.

"I call it Snackers," Chef Claire said as she opened the bag she was holding.

"Chef Claire is dabbling in dog food," I said, opening my bag and glancing down at Chloe who was sitting on her haunches and staring up at me.

"It's a dog granola," Chef Claire said, starting to feed small handfuls to Al and Dente. "I've got two versions. One is grain free, but this one has wheat and oatmeal, sweet potato, apples, carrots, and chicken jerky along with a few other goodies. My guys love it."

Missy began feeding bites to her three labs, and they wagged their tails furiously. Captain woofed loudly. I looked down at the dog who was staring at Josie then glanced over at her just as she was tossing a handful into her mouth.

"You're unbelievable," I said, giving her a sad shake of the head.

"What can I say? It's fantastic," she said, reaching into the bag.

"Hey, that's for the dogs," Chef Claire said, laughing.

"There's plenty to go around," Josie said as she watched Captain devour the large handful she was holding out. "You don't mind sharing, do you, Captain?"

Captain woofed his displeasure.

"What a good boy," I said, rubbing the dog's head. "You tell her."

Chapter 18

As I expected, all seven dogs were soon sprawled out in the bow sound asleep and softly snoring. We all headed to the stern where the rest of the group was snacking and sipping wine, except for Trudy and Charlotte who were still pounding Kamikazes and getting louder by the minute. I built a small nosh plate of egg rolls and assorted deli items and sat down between Josie and Chef Claire. Jessie was having a quiet conversation with Missy, and my mom was doing an amazing job of feigning interest in whatever Jill's mother was babbling about. I spotted Jill sitting by herself staring out at the water, eventually made eye contact, and raised my glass to her in a silent toast. She gave me a small smile, returned the toast, then her eyes drifted back out over the water. Faith was also sitting by herself with her legs tucked under her and an angry, frozen glare that looked like it had been etched on.

"What's up with Beelzebub?" I said.

"She's looked like that since she sat down," Josie said. "I don't think she's a big fan of being out on the River."

"One more reason to hate her."

"Exactly," Josie said, sneaking a peek over at Faith. "She sure looks like she wants to kill somebody."

"She's probably still mad you pushed her in the water," I said with a grin.

"For the last time, she fell in. What's the deal with Jessie?" Josie whispered.

"She seems like a good kid," I whispered back. "But she's obviously had a rough life. She was orphaned at six, then bounced around foster homes until she started college."

"Poor kid," Josie said softly, then leaned in closer. "And?"

"And she'd been sleeping with him," I said.

"Interesting. Eternal love?"

"No, not even close. I think it was more of a notch in the belt kind of thing."

"The pig," Josie said, shaking her head in disgust.

"No, a notch in the belt for her. Not him."

"Really?" Josie whispered with a frown. "Well, I suppose it can cut both ways. The young student becomes infatuated with an older man and decides to see if it's worth it."

"You ever do it?"

"What? The notch in the belt thing?"

"Yeah."

"And ruin a perfectly good belt?" she deadpanned.

I laughed loud enough to draw the attention of the others.

"Don't mind me," I said, waving it off. "Josie was just sharing a fashion tip."

"Make sure you take good notes, darling."

"Funny, Mom."

"What time is he supposed to call?" Josie whispered.

"It should be any minute now," I said, glancing at my watch that read a quarter to three.

"Do you really think this is going to work?"

"I don't know. It's kinda like fishing," I said. "You try to pick the best spot and use the bait you think is going to work, but, at some point, you just have to toss your line in the water and wait for something to bite."

"Except if this thing blows up, you won't be the bait. You'll be the one left flopping on the bank with a mouthful of cyanide."

"Nothing gets past you," I said, gently punching her on the shoulder.

My phone buzzed, and I answered quickly.

"This is Suzy."

"Chief Abrams reporting for duty," he said. "I've got you on speaker. Detective Williams is here with me."

"Oh, hi, Chief Abrams," I said, loud enough for everyone on the boat to hear. "What's up?"

"You said to call you around three, so here I am. What do you feel like talking about? How about the weather? Low seventies, gentle breeze out of the west. It must be a gorgeous day to be out on the River. Or maybe you'd like to discuss your love life? But I guess that would be a very short conversation... Are you having fun yet?"

"No," I said softly, squeezing the phone a bit tighter.

"This is going to be great," the Chief said, laughing. "I get to say anything I want, and all you'll be able to do is grin and bear it."

"I guess we'll see about that, Chief," I said casually as I glanced around the boat. "I see. That's very good news."

"Did you know I went to the zoo the other day?" the Chief said.

"Really?" I said. "You have been busy."

"And the only thing in the zoo was a single dog," the Chief said.

"Okay."

"Yeah, it was a Shih Tzu," he said, roaring with laughter.

"I'm not sure I understand," I said into the phone. It was true, I didn't get the joke.

"Think about it," the Chief said.

"Oh, okay. Now I understand," I said as my neurons finally made the connection. I shook my head and switched the phone to my other ear. "Today, really? I'm surprised."

"A dog walks into a bar and orders a martini," the Chief said.

"Uh-huh," I said, nodding as I glanced around at everyone who continued to watch me closely.

"And the bartender puts the martini down on the bar and tells the dog it's twenty bucks. Then the bartender says, you know we don't get many dogs in here."

"At those prices, I'm not surprised," I blurted.

"Oh, you've heard it," the Chief said. "Then how about this one? What do you call a dog magician? ...Are you trying to figure it out?

"No."

"You're just wondering how you can manage to work *labracadabrador* into the conversation, aren't you?"

"Yup."

"I'll be here all week," he said, laughing.

"Well, thanks for the call, Chief," I said, making a mental note to make him pay for his little stunt. "Yes, they're all here on the boat. Yes, I'm sure they'll be very happy to hear the good news."

"Suzy?" the Chief said, turning serious.

"Yes?"

"We're meeting with Henrietta at six-thirty in her office," he said. "She wants to go over everything again we talked about on the phone. Try not to be late."

"Got it. Thanks for calling, Chief."

I put my phone away and glanced around.

"As I'm sure you heard, that was Chief Abrams. He just got a call from Upstate Medical."

"You mentioned something about good news?" Jill's mother said.

"Yes, Bill came out of his coma early this morning," I said. "And he's being discharged from intensive care."

I waited several seconds for the comments and sighs of relief to finish, then continued.

"He's being transferred back to the Clay Bay hospital as we speak," I said.

"What?" Faith said, frowning. "How is that possible? The guy just came out of a coma."

"Apparently, Upstate is at capacity and needs the bed. And his doctor said that Bill was okay to make the trip. His vitals are all good, and the doctor thinks that in a few days he might even be able to go home."

"Is he talking yet?" Jill's mother said, leaning forward.

"No, according to what the Chief heard, he's still pretty out of it. And they're going to keep him in isolation tonight just to be safe. But there's a good chance he'll be lucid in the morning. Maybe even able to handle some visitors."

"I don't get it," Faith said, shaking her head. "Something about this doesn't seem right."

"I would have thought you'd be happy your father was going to recover," Jennifer said, glaring at her daughter.

"I am happy," Faith snapped.

"That's her happy face? Geez, no wonder she's still single," Josie whispered as she leaned closer.

"You're one to talk."

"Hey, at least I *have* a happy face," she said, her voice rising a notch.

"Shhh," I whispered. "I want to hear this."

"That's amazing," Charlotte said, draining what was left of her drink. "He's one tough son of a gun, huh?"

"Apparently," Trudy said, reaching for the pitcher of Kamikazes. "And incredibly lucky."

"What was that comment about prices, darling?"

"Oh, Chief Abrams was just talking about how much the bill is going to be for two nights in the ICU," I said, lying through my teeth.

"Well, I'm sure not paying it," Jennifer said, scowling.

"Nobody expects you to pay his hospital bill, Mom," Jill said.

"I'm just saying."

"Have they been able to confirm he was poisoned?" Missy said.

"They have," I said, nodding. "They found trace amounts of cyanide."

"Only trace amounts?" Faith said, frowning. "How the heck could that have happened?"

"I'm not sure I understand your question," I said, staring at her.

"Me either," Missy said.

Faith caught the looks everyone was giving her and flushed red with embarrassment.

"I'm just wondering how he only got a small dose," she said, recovering quickly. "Obviously, whoever tried to poison him didn't do a very good job."

"Don't worry. I'm sure whoever did it will do a better job the next time, right, Faith?" Missy said, glaring at her.

"What's that supposed to mean?" Faith said.

"I thought I was perfectly clear," Missy said, then took a sip of wine.

"Whatever you say, *Godmother*," Faith said, giving Missy her death-stare.

"Drop it, Faith," Jill said.

"Yeah, the little princess and her fairy godmother," Faith said, shaking her head as she glanced over at her sister. "You get the hotshot professor. I'm stuck with Madame Kamikaze over there."

"Faith, stop it!" Jennifer said. "I'm so sorry, Charlotte. She didn't mean that."

"Like hell I didn't," Faith said, glaring at her mother. "Why do you care what I say about her? You two hate each other's guts."

"Wow," Charlotte said, shaking her head. "What a gene pool. This family should come with a warning label."

"Psychiatrist not on duty. Swim at your own risk," Josie whispered as she tried to follow all the action.

"Shhhh," I said, stifling a laugh.

"That's enough," Jennifer snapped at her family, then she focused on my mother. "I'm so sorry. You go to all this trouble to give us a wonderful day on the River, and this is how we repay you."

"Don't worry about it," my mother said, patting her hand. "It's completely understandable. You're all dealing with an enormous amount of stress."

I gave my mother an admiring stare. Talk about remaining calm in the teeth of a storm. I was on the edge of my seat and about two seconds away from punching Faith's lights out then tossing her overboard. But I doubt if I could have beaten Josie to the other side of the boat.

"Yeah," Charlotte said, taking a sip of her fresh drink. "Stress. That must be it."

"I'm not stressed at all," Faith said. "Just bored out of my mind."

"Will you please just shut your mouth," Jill said, staring in disbelief at her sister.

A tense, hushed silence fell over the boat, then I nudged Josie, and we headed for the bow to play with the dogs. They were still sleeping soundly and barely stirred. But we did receive several tail thumps that echoed softly off the fiberglass deck. My mother followed us, and I draped an arm over her shoulder.

"How do you do it, Mom?"

"Do what, darling?"

"Keep your cool like that."

"That was nothing," she said, shrugging. "You should see what goes on at some of the town council meetings." She glanced back at Faith who continued to glare at everything, yet nothing in particular. "She is a vile human being."

"She certainly is," Josie said.

"Do you think she's the killer?" my mother said.

"She's got my vote," Josie said.

"No, I don't," I said, shaking my head.

"Really?" my mother said, frowning. "With that temper?"

"She's not smart enough to have done it," I said, finally saying out loud what had been running through my head for the past hour. "Those murders required planning and a fair amount of calculated risk. I don't think Faith could have pulled that off. Like her father always said, her elevator doesn't run all the way to the top floor."

"So, you think you know who the killer is?" my mother said.

"I do," I said, nodding as I drifted off.

"There she goes," Josie said, laughing.

"Darling?"

"Yes, Mom?"

"Are you going to tell us?"

"No, I need to clear up a few things first," I said, continuing to squint into the distance.

"Darling, are you all right?"

"I'm fine, Mom," I said, returning to the moment and giving her a hug.

"Good. Let's see if we can keep it that way tonight, okay?" my mother said.

"I'll be fine," I said, for the first time believing my own words. "But we should get going. I have a meeting at six-thirty."

"With who?" my mother said.

"The Chief, Detective Williams, and Henrietta."

"Make sure you get fitted for a large gown," Josie said. "For maximum coverage and all that."

"Thanks for the tip," I said, making a face at her.

"Hey, it's the least I can do," Josie said, beaming at me with an enormous grin. Then she pointed at her mouth. "Now, this is a happy face."

Chapter 19

Henrietta Calhoun, like my mother, was an elegant older woman who took great pride in her appearance as well as her ability to remain active and keep making a meaningful contribution to the community. But while my mother was a *dabbler* who liked to stick her fingers and, in my case, her nose into as many things as possible, Henrietta's primary focus was on the preservation and expansion of the Clay Bay hospital. I'd known her since I was a young girl, and I'd recently joined my mother as one of the biggest donors to the hospital's foundation, and regularly helped out with many of their fundraising efforts.

As a small-town hospital, it couldn't offer the wide range of services and specialties common in large, urban medical centers, but what our local hospital did, it did extremely well. The place was perched on a hill overlooking the River and over the years had been the target of developers with designs on turning the property into a high-end hotel and relocating the hospital to an area of town where the views weren't nearly as spectacular, and the price per square foot was, from the developer's perspective, more appropriate for a community asset that operated on a non-profit basis. But Henrietta, with the support of the vast majority of local residents, had successfully beaten back every attempt, and all of the prospective developers had skulked away after learning a very valuable lesson: Don't mess with Henrietta Calhoun.

Thirty years into her career as administrator, Henrietta continued to watch over the operations of the hospital like a protective mama-mallard keeping a close eye on her ducklings, and she wasn't shy about taking a nip out of anyone who threatened to disrupt its clockwork efficiency. As such, I was initially concerned about the possibility of her taking a big bite out of me when I arrived for our scheduled meeting. But it soon became apparent that instead of cranky, Henrietta was merely curious about my intentions.

Actually, baffled is probably the more accurate term.

"How do you manage to keep getting yourself into these messes, Suzy?" Henrietta said as she sat back in her desk chair and stared at me over the top of her steepled fingers.

"Yeah, I know," I said, shrugging. "I really need to start working on that."

"This one seems especially…creative," she said, raising an eyebrow at me.

"My mother's been coaching you, hasn't she?" I said, reaching into my overnight satchel for a fresh bag of bite-sized.

"No," she said, laughing as she reached for a small handful of the chocolate delights from the bag I was holding out. "I came up with that one all by myself."

I offered the bag of bite-sized to Chief Abrams and Detective Williams who were sitting on either side of me, but they waved it away.

"I had a hard time believing what you were telling me over the phone, so I thought it would be a good idea for us to meet face to face," Henrietta said, already unwrapping her second bite-sized.

"So you can try to talk me out of it, right?" I said, reaching back into the bag. Then I noticed both men watching me unwrap and toss the chocolate morsels into my mouth with machine-like proficiency. "I missed dinner."

"Suzy, I've known you since you were barely old enough to hold your own fishing pole," Henrietta said, gesturing for me to move the bag closer. She grabbed another small handful. "I know better than waste my energy trying to talk you out of something once you've made up your mind. But I am trying to run a hospital here, so I'm sure you can understand my concern."

"Sure, sure," I said, nodding as I swallowed. "But don't worry, Henrietta. You and your staff won't even know we're here."

"And why is that?" she said, unwrapping another bite-sized.

"Because we're going to be over in the east wing in room one," I said.

"The east wing?" she said, frowning. "The east wing is closed."

"I know," I said, nodding. "Hence, my comment about how you won't even know we're there."

"But that whole area is about to become a construction zone," Henrietta said.

"I'm very aware of that, Henrietta," I said, remembering the number of trailing zeroes on the check I'd recently written to help fund the renovation.

"Yes, of course," she said, nodding. "And thanks again for the check. That was very generous of you and your mother."

"We were happy to do it," I said, tossing the bag of bite-sized back into my satchel.

"I have a question," Henrietta said.

"Only one?" Chief Abrams said, glancing over at me.

I made a face at him then looked back across the desk at Henrietta.

"How will the killer, assuming for a moment that this person does actually show up, know you're going to be in the east wing?"

"Good question," the Chief said, glancing over at Detective Williams. "Is that one on your list, too?"

"It is," the detective said.

"I sort of let it slip on the ride back today that Bill was going to be there," I said. "We were chatting about his condition, and I just tossed it out."

"Well, since this whole thing is basically a fishing expedition, why stop now, right?" the Chief said.

"But that whole area is shut down," Henrietta said. "Won't the killer be suspicious?"

"Nah," I said, shaking my head. "I seriously doubt it. The killer's not a local and wouldn't know the difference. And if you just leave a few lights on in the hallway, I doubt if she'll give it a second thought."

Henrietta began to gently rock back and forth in her chair deep in thought. Then she glanced back and forth at the two cops.

"And you guys are comfortable with this?" she said.

"Define comfortable," Chief Abrams said.

"You're really not funny, Chief," I said, brushing my hair back from my face, annoyed.

"Relax, Suzy," he said softly. "We've gone back and forth dozens of times about it, Henrietta. And while it's definitely odd, in all honesty, we haven't been able to come up with anything better."

"Thank you," I said, pouting.

"Not that we think it's going to pay off," the Chief said. "But I'm sure we'll be able to keep Suzy safe."

"No one from my staff will be within two hundred feet of the east wing," she said. "You do know that, right?"

"I do," the Chief said.

Henrietta nodded then focused on Detective Williams.

"And you're okay going ahead with this plan as well?" she said.

"Oh, I'm getting overtime, so I'm totally cool with it," the detective deadpanned.

I did a slow burn as I waited out the laughter.

"If this person does show up, what are your plans to apprehend her?" Henrietta said, glancing down at what I assumed was a list of questions she had jotted down.

"The Chief and I will be in the room with Suzy the entire time. And we'll have six undercover state cops stationed at various exits outside," Detective Williams said. "And don't worry, they'll be under strict orders not to shoot unless it's to return fire."

"That won't be a problem," I said, shaking my head. "She's not a shooter."

"She's not? You're saying you know who the killer is?" Henrietta said, staring at me.

"Yeah, I think I do," I said, nodding.

"Then why don't you just arrest her now and save us all the headache?"

"We can't do that," Detective Williams said. "We don't have any proof."

"You don't have any proof, but you're sure you know who it is?" Henrietta said, leaning forward and placing her elbows on her desk.

"Yes, we are," I said.

Both Chief Abrams and the detective cleared their throats.

"Well, I'm sure," I said. "These two aren't convinced yet."

"I see," she said, leaning back and resuming her rocking. "And you're convinced it has to happen tonight?"

"Yes, she believes that Bill is going be able to start talking in the morning. And that's something she can't let happen."

"I see." Henrietta stared off deep in thought. Then she slowly nodded. "Okay, I'll play. But just for tonight. That's it. And if this blows up in my face, Suzy, I'm going to hunt you down."

"I have no doubt about it, Henrietta," I said, flashing her a smile.

"But promise me you won't do anything stupid and get yourself hurt," she said.

"Well, if I do, I'll be in the perfect place to deal with it, huh?"

"That's not funny," she said, giving me a blank stare.

"Really? I kinda liked it," I said, shrugging. I glanced back and forth between the Chief and Detective Williams. "Okay, I think we're all set."

"There's just one more thing," Henrietta said, completely focused on me.

"What's that?" I said, frowning as I returned her stare.

"What size gown do you need?" she deadpanned. "Personally, I'd go with the large for maximum coverage."

"Forget it," I said, shaking my head. "I'm not wearing one of-" I stopped and glared at her. "Josie called you, didn't she?"

"No," Henrietta said, laughing. "It was your mother. But I think Josie put her up to it."

Chapter 20

Henrietta escorted us out of her office, and we followed her down a long hallway, made a right, then another, and we were soon standing outside a closed door with a nameplate that read E1 in the deserted east wing. She flipped a light switch, and the overhead fluorescents flickered along the length of the hallway then held. The lighting was dim, but I could easily make out the expression on Chief Abrams and Detective William's faces. It was pretty much the standard cop stare, but I thought I noticed a touch of mild amusement mixed in. I glanced around and nodded my approval at what I thought was an accurate depiction of how a hospital patient area should look like in the middle of the night.

"I think this works just fine," the Chief said.

"It should," Henrietta said. "It's the lighting we've had in this wing for the past twenty years."

"Thanks so much for your help, Henrietta," I said, giving her a hug.

"Oh, I sure hope you know what you're doing, Suzy," she said, squeezing me tight, then glancing back and forth at both cops. "Call me. Either way, as soon as anything happens."

"Will do," the Chief said. "Thanks, Henrietta. I know you're going way out on a limb here for us."

"Oh, I'll be fine," she said, chuckling. "Mrs. C. is the board chairperson. She'll be the one who'll have to do all the explaining. Suzy's *her* daughter. I just work here."

For some reason, she found her comment funny, and her laughter echoed as she waved goodbye and headed back down the hall toward her office. I slowly opened the door and turned on the lights. One hospital bed, stripped down, dominated the room, and I noticed the bathroom on the other side of the room. I headed for the closet and found a stack of sheets and pillowcases.

"Either one of you know how to make a hospital corner?" I said, holding out the sheets.

"Nice try," Chief Abrams said, laughing. "You can make your own bed."

"Add a *young lady,* and you know who you'd sound like, right?"

"I do," the Chief said. "And I'm sure your mother would agree with me."

Detective Williams and Chief Abrams sat down and watched me make the bed. When I finished, it looked a lot like my bed did at home right after I'd made it. Which is to say, pretty much like a collection of dirty laundry with a sheet draped over it. But I decided it wouldn't make any difference after the lights were out, and I shrugged it off. I walked into the bathroom, motioned for both of them to follow me and bring their chairs with them. They positioned the chairs just inside the bathroom near the open door, and I turned the bathroom light off.

"How's that?" I said.

"Dark," the Chief said.

I flipped the light back on and made a face at him.

"Don't worry, we'll be able to follow all the action from here," he said, then glanced at his watch. "Okay, it's going to be dark soon, so let's turn the lights off and get you into bed." He draped a leg over his knee. "How the heck did you figure out the stuff about the girl?"

"It just came to me on the boat," I said. "Jessie was telling me the story about how her parents had died in a plane crash and then said she spent several years bouncing around foster homes. At first, I didn't give it a second thought. But then I started wondering why the daughter of a successful aircraft designer would end up the foster care system. Her parents must have had a boatload of money."

"They did," Chief Abrams said. "And huge insurance policies on both of them."

"And since money wasn't an issue, even if Jessie didn't have any family, it shouldn't have been that hard to find a family friend or somebody who worked for her dad's company to take care of her. I don't understand why she felt the need to concoct the foster kid story."

"Maybe she felt abandoned and imagining herself as a foster kid fit the narrative," Detective Williams said.

"Well, she certainly had a lot of time to work up her story," Chief Abrams said, then looked at me. "How did you know she'd been institutionalized the whole time?"

"I didn't," I said, shaking my head. "I sort of took a flyer on that one. But it kind of made sense once I landed on the idea. If she had grown up in another family, by now, she'd be calling them mom and dad, and probably telling all sorts of stories about her childhood. Since she doesn't, and once you rule out foster kid, her being institutionalized is one of the few remaining options. I can't believe you tracked all that down in a couple of hours."

"If she didn't have a record, we'd still be looking," Detective Williams said.

"What did she do?" I said.

"On her sixteenth birthday, she took off and stole a car," he said. "The guy who runs the institution said they'd just started talking about the prospect of releasing her. He thinks she did it because she was afraid of being out in society all by herself and panicked. I can see that."

"Sort of like a long-term prisoner who finally makes parole," Chief Abrams said. "A lot of times those guys just can't handle it, and they'll do something to get themselves put right back in."

"Yeah," Detective Williams said, nodding. "After she got caught with the car, apparently, she settled down and was the model kid."

"And they let her out when she turned eighteen?" I said, still trying to fit all the pieces together.

"They did," Detective Williams said. "Her doctors felt she was well enough to handle it, and she had her sponsor on the outside who promised to keep a close eye on her."

"Some sponsor," I said.

"Yeah," Detective Williams said. "But since she had a big trust fund and been accepted into college, the guy said they'd pretty much run out of reasons to keep her there."

"Being nuts isn't enough of a reason these days?" the Chief said, frowning.

"The doctor says she isn't crazy," Detective Williams said. "Present evidence to the contrary notwithstanding."

"Then she decides to spend the summer here and gets caught up in this mess," I said, shaking my head. "I kind of feel sorry for her."

"Yeah, the whole thing makes me sad," the Chief said. "But I guess watching your parents fall out of the sky when you're six-years-old might make your wires cross."

"Absolutely," I said.

"So, what's your excuse?" the Chief said, grinning at me.

"Funny."

"This is definitely one of the weirder ones," the Chief said, then he glanced at Detective Williams. "Have you ever done a stakeout like this before?"

"Hiding in the bathroom of a deserted hospital room waiting for someone to show up and kill a woman who's pretending to be a guy who's already dead? No, Chief, I gotta say that this is a first."

"Yeah, me too," the Chief said. "The things we do for the job, right?"

"You got that right," Detective Williams deadpanned. "The least she could have done was wear the gown."

"I know. That might have almost made it worthwhile missing the hockey game tonight."

"Yeah, Bruins-Canadiens. It's been a heck of a series," the detective said.

"Are you two done?" I said, staring at them, then had a thought. "Hey, what do you mean, *almost*?"

"It's game seven," the Chief said, shrugging.

Detective Williams snorted.

"I'm going to bed," I said, walking away, then stopping to look back over my shoulder. "Fully clothed in case you were wondering."

"The thought never crossed my mind," Detective Williams said.

I climbed into bed then pulled the blanket up to my chin with my arms underneath the covers.

"What do you think?" I said, glancing at them sitting in the bathroom.

"It's a very sexy look," the Chief said. "Colonial Amish, right?"

"Everybody's a comedian," I snapped. "Just turn the lights off."

I was soon cocooned in complete darkness, and the reality of what I was doing struck me like a bolt of lightning. My neurons were on fire, and I felt the unmistakable surge of fear flow through my entire body. I focused on my breathing, felt a bit better, but decided I was going to need additional help to get through my self-imposed encounter with insanity.

The killer's, not my own.

There'd be plenty of time to worry about my own issues later on. Assuming I managed to survive.

I fumbled underneath the covers and located what I was searching for. A few moments later, I heard Detective Williams' voice come from the bathroom.

"I think I heard something," he whispered.

"Shhhh," the Chief whispered. "Let's give it a second...Okay, got it. I know what that is."

Then he spoke a bit louder, and I couldn't miss the fatherly tone in his voice.

"Suzy?"

"Yeah?"

"Please put the bag of bite-sized away."

"Okay."

"Thank you."

"Sorry."

"It's a little late for that wouldn't you say?"

Chapter 21

In the darkness, my neurons continued to fire and wander off in several different directions. But after I forced myself to focus, I eventually landed on three possible outcomes that could play themselves out tonight. The worst, of course, was the possibility that I might die of cyanide poisoning. But I put the probability of that happening no higher than five percent; ten tops. Two experienced cops were sitting ten feet away, and Chief Abrams knew for a fact that if anything bad happened to me, my mother would make his life miserable. Which made perfect sense since she'd need someone to take her anger and frustration out on, and I wouldn't be around to bear the brunt of what was sure to be an endless, brutal harangue.

The second outcome was the very real possibility that the murderer wouldn't show up thereby leaving me completely vulnerable to the taunts and laughter of all my friends and acquaintances. The story of me in a hospital bed waiting to catch a killer would be evoked, embellished, and retold at every Thanksgiving dinner and Christmas, not to mention every other time someone just happened to remember it. By the time the story was being retold for the tenth time, I was sure I'd be wearing a low-cut, micro-gown and fire-red lipstick with a come-hither look. As I laid there dreaming up possible story elements, option one began to look better by the minute.

The final possible outcome was that the killer would actually show up and Chief Abrams and Detective Williams would quickly and efficiently subdue her. And I would be carried off on their shoulders as the conquering hero. But before

I could even start working on my victory speech, I got sleepy and nodded off.

When I woke up, at first, I had no idea where I was or how long I'd been asleep. But that was least of my problems. I heard the door open partway, and a stream of dim light from the hallway spilled into the room. I froze in bed with my eyes wide open staring up at the ceiling. Then the door clicked shut, and I was again surrounded by darkness. Soft footsteps approached the bed, and I had to force myself to keep breathing. The footsteps stopped, and I sensed her presence only a few feet away.

"What am I gonna do with you, Bill?" she whispered. "Leave it to you to screw up a perfectly good murder."

I was glad I was under the covers in the dark. I was shaking like a leaf and positive the bed was doing the same.

"How you managed to spit that gumdrop out I'll never know. I was sure I'd shoved it all the way down," she said. "But let's see if we can get it right this time, shall we?"

I felt the chill the cold night air had left on her as she leaned closer, and I couldn't miss the minty smell of her breath. Then she crunched and swallowed what was left of the mint. I heard the soft rustle of what I assumed was her rummaging through her pockets.

"I suppose I could just stuff this down your throat with my fingers," she whispered with a slight mumble. "But since you always loved the way I kissed you, how about one more for old-time sake? Pucker up, Billy boy."

"I'm sorry, Missy, but you're really not my type."

Missy screamed loud enough to pop an eardrum, and the lights came on. Missy stared down at me, wild-eyed, then glanced behind her and saw Chief Abrams and Detective Williams standing in the bathroom doorway, their guns drawn.

"Suzy?" she said, staring down at me.

"Nothing gets past you."

Missy gagged briefly, then spat out whatever she had in her mouth and bolted for the door just as both cops came out of the bathroom. At least they would have if they hadn't tried to exit through the door at exactly the same time. Their shoulders got wedged in the doorway for a few seconds, and Missy raced out of the room, and I heard her footsteps until they faded.

"Really?" I said, glaring at the two cops when they finally made their way out of the bathroom. "Nice work. You guys only had to do one simple thing."

"Shut it," Chief Abrams said on his way out of the room.

"Just stay here," Detective Williams said as he followed the Chief out the door and down the hall.

"Yeah, like that's gonna happen," I said, shaking my head as I climbed out of bed.

I did my best slow lumber down the hall, and a few moments later I saw both of them standing near the main entrance talking on their radios.

"What do you mean you didn't see her?" Detective Williams said.

"Jimmy," the Chief said. "You got anything? Okay, hang tight. I'll get back to you in a minute."

"Are you kidding me?" Detective Williams said, shaking his head. "All right, just stay there and keep an eye on her car."

They both lowered their radios and stared at each other, bewildered.

"I don't believe it," Detective Williams said. "Where the heck did she go?"

Henrietta approached at a brisk pace. She came to a stop and glanced back and forth at us obviously waiting for an explanation.

"Don't look at me," I snapped. "Talk to the Fife twins."

"I said, shut it," the Chief said, glaring at me.

"She was ten feet away. And there were two of you," I said, shaking my head. "Unfreakingbelievable."

"How would you like to spend the night in jail?" the Chief said.

"On what charge?" I said, returning his glare. "Impersonating a cop? No wait, that's your thing."

"Maybe I'll just lock you up to teach you some manners, *young lady*."

"Nice try, Chief. But you need to lower your voice a notch and say it slower," I said, making a face at him. Then I stared off into the distance shaking my head. "Unfreakingbelievable."

"Would one of you care to explain what's going on?" Henrietta said, her patience rapidly disappearing. "I heard one of the emergency exit alarms go off."

"She got away," Detective Williams said.

"The killer actually showed up?" Henrietta said, baffled.

"Yeah, she did," the Chief said.

"How on earth did she escape?" she said.

Detective Williams and Chief Abrams exchanged chagrined looks with each other.

"We sort of got stuck in the door coming out of the bathroom," the Chief said softly. "And she got out of the room and ran down the hall."

"No, I don't think she went down the hall," I said, shaking my head. "The footsteps didn't last long enough."

"Well, nobody has seen her outside," Detective Williams said. "And her car is still parked out front."

"Maybe somebody picked her up in a different car," the Chief said.

"No, my guys would have seen it."

"It's not a car," I said, heading for the glass doors directly across from the entrance. "Come on."

"Where are you going?" the Chief said.

"Down to the dock," I said, pushing the double doors open. "She's going by boat."

"Boat?" Detective Williams said.

"We have a dock off the front of the hospital we use for patients arriving by boat," Henrietta said, by way of explanation. "Just follow the path down."

"I know where the dock is, Henrietta," the Chief said, annoyed.

"There's no need to get snarky with me, Chief."

"Just try not to trip over each other on the way down," I said, over my shoulder as I broke into my fastest lumber.

Despite my best efforts, both cops soon passed me with ease, and by the time I caught up with them they were standing in bright light under a metal lamppost that was bolted into the dock and scanning the water for signs of a boat. I bent over and took several deep breaths.

"Are you okay?" the Chief said, giving me a quick once-over.

"I'll...be fine," I said, standing upright. "Man, I really need to get to the gym. You see anything?"

"No, it's pretty dark out there," Detective Williams said.

"Well, it is night," I snapped, still extremely annoyed with both cops.

"You can drop the attitude, Suzy," the detective said, pointing downriver to his right. "Hang on. What's that?"

"That is what's called a boat, Detective," I said.

"You're really starting to annoy me."

"Well, you're not doing much for my mood, either. So let's call it even," I said, then frowned at the approaching vessel. "That's Rooster's boat."

"It certainly is," the Chief said, heading to the other end of the dock to meet the boat.

Rooster idled the boat next to the dock, and he grinned up at us. Titan, his German Shepherd who rarely left his side, was sitting next to him.

"Well, I know this isn't a greeting party," Rooster said. "Don't tell me she got away."

"Yeah, she escaped," Detective Williams said. "Hey, how did you know what we were doing?"

"Small town," Rooster said with a shrug. "You let her get away? How the heck did you manage to do that? There's two of you."

"You might not want to go there, Rooster. It's a bit of a sore spot," I said, kneeling down to pet the German Shepherd. "Hey, Titan. Who's the good boy?" I rubbed the dog's head, then stood up and arched my back that was beginning to cramp.

"We think she used a boat to get away," Detective Williams said, staring back out at the water.

"I'm sure you're right," Rooster said, nodding.

"How do you know that?"

"Because somebody just stole one of my rentals," Rooster said.

"And you followed the boat here?" Detective Williams said.

"Unfreakingbelievable," I mumbled under my breath, but still loud enough for the cop to hear me.

"Why else would I be out here in the middle of the night?"

"Don't ask them to think, Rooster. You'll only confuse them," I said. "Did you see who it was?"

"I didn't get a good look," he said. "But it was definitely a woman."

"Jessie," I said, then glanced around for confirmation.

"It has to be her," the Chief said. "Well, they don't know their way around the River, so my guess is that they'll pull into shore someplace nearby. Maybe they have a second car parked somewhere on the edge of town."

"They won't be going very far right away," I said, reaching for my phone.

"Why on earth not?" Detective Williams said.

"Because I have her dogs. She won't leave town without them."

"Why not?" the detective said, staring at me.

"You're not a dog person, are you, Detective Williams?"

"No, I'm more of a cat guy," he said, shrugging.

"That's not the only reason she isn't going far," Rooster said.

We all looked at him and waited for him to continue.

"Oh, that's right," I said, grinning at Rooster.

"They'll be running out of gas in the very near future," Rooster said, scratching one of Titan's ears.

"I'm surrounded by savants," Detective Williams said, exasperated. "How on earth do you know that?"

"Because I always make sure my rentals have just enough gas in them to get them out on the water, but not far enough to get away."

"And that makes it easy to catch the thieves and have them arrested," Detective Williams said, nodding.

"Man, you're on fire tonight, Detective," I deadpanned. "Pity you didn't show a bit more of that flash earlier."

"Suzy, will you just let it go?" the Chief snapped.

"You'd like that wouldn't you?" I said, dialing the number and putting the phone on speaker.

"Hey, you're alive," Josie said. "That's good news. What's up?"

"Well, she showed up," I said, then glared at both cops. "Then she got away."

"She got away? How the heck did she do that? There's two of them," Josie said, obviously surprised.

"I'd let them speak for themselves, but I doubt if they feel like explaining at the moment."

"Oh, they're there with you? Hi, Chief, Detective Williams."

They both mumbled hellos.

"Hey, Josie."

"Rooster, what are you doing there?" Josie said.

"Oh, just the usual. I'm trying to hunt down a stolen boat," Rooster said.

"Did somebody steal one of your rentals again?"

"Yeah."

"Well, they won't get far, right?" Josie said, laughing. "Hey, don't forget. Titan is due for his shots."

"I'll bring him in next week," Rooster said.

"Are we about done with the chit-chat?" Detective Williams said. "It's really cold out here."

"I wouldn't worry about it, Detective. I doubt you could even *catch* a cold," I said.

"How many years do you think I'd get for shooting an unarmed civilian?" Detective Williams said to the Chief.

"At least twenty," the Chief said. "Unless the judge considered the mitigating factors."

"Mitigating factors?"

"Her," the Chief said, nodding in my direction.

I made a face at him then focused on the phone.

"Did you get a phone call?"

"Yup, just like you said she would, Missy called about an hour ago and said she'd be stopping by to pick up the labs."

"Did you take them down to the Inn and put them in one of the condos?"

"I did. And they are currently resting comfortably with Rocky and Bullwinkle," Josie said.

"Good call."

"Rocky and Bullwinkle?" Detective Williams said, raising an eyebrow.

"Our nighttime security guards," I said.

"You have two guys working dog security?" the detective said, confused.

"No, two Rottweilers," I said, then spoke to Josie. "Don't worry, I doubt if she's going to get a chance to get over there. But to be safe, just stay up at the house. I'll ask Detective Williams to send a car over to keep an eye on the Inn. If Missy does show up, she won't get within twenty feet of her dogs."

"Yeah, Rocky and Bullwinkle get pretty cranky when they're woken up in the middle of the night," Josie said. "Hey, does this mean we're going to be able to keep the labs?"

"Geez, I hadn't thought about that," I said. "Yeah, I guess it might."

"Oh, no. Not the briar patch," Josie said, laughing.

"What do you think? Would we put them up for adoption or just keep them as part of the family?"

"I'd love to keep them, but if we found the perfect family for them, that would be good, too."

"But we have to keep them together," Josie said. "There's no way we could split them up."

"No, of course not. That wouldn't be fair to them."

"Who are you people?" Detective Williams said to no one in particular.

"Why don't you folks hop in the boat, and we'll go on a little scouting mission," Rooster said.

"It's a little dark, isn't it?" Detective Williams said.

"Not with this," Rooster said, flipping on a searchlight that hit the detective right in the eyes. "Oh, sorry about that, Detective."

Detective Williams shielded his eyes, waved the searchlight away, then climbed into the boat. He flinched when Titan turned around to sniff him, and he stood very still in the middle of the boat and kept a close eye on the dog.

"Look, I gotta run," I said. "I'm going to be hungry when I get home. Is there anything left?"

"I put a pretty good dent in the Shepherd's Pie, but there's plenty left."

"Good. Later."

"Be careful."

I slipped my phone back in my pocket and followed Chief Abrams into the boat.

"Which way do you think they went?" Detective Williams said, glancing up and down the River.

"I'm going to guess that way," Rooster said, pointing upriver.

"Why?"

"Because if they went the other way, there's a good chance they'd end back at my place," Rooster said.

"Good thinking," Detective Williams said, nodding and pointing upriver. "Yeah, let's go that way."

"Unfreakingbelievable."

Chapter 22

Instead of driving slow and sweeping the waterline with the searchlight, Rooster roared away from the dock. The Chief and I, as veteran River Rats, were accustomed to rapid acceleration on the water, and we both held onto the side of the boat for support when the boat surged forward. However, Detective Williams was standing in the middle of the boat with nothing to hold onto, and he tumbled backward and ended up flat on his back against the transom. Rooster glanced over his shoulder when he heard the noise, but didn't slow down. Detective Williams got to his feet, then slowly inched his way toward the bow after the boat had planed.

"Aren't you going a little fast for a search effort?" the Detective said, struggling to make himself heard above the roar of the engine.

"Yup," Rooster said, nodding without slowing down.

"Okay, thanks for clearing that up," the detective said, shaking his head.

"He's going upriver until he's sure the boat is downriver from us," I yelled. "Once they're out of gas, the current is going to grab them and they'll starting drifting back toward town."

"Wouldn't the boat have oars or a paddle?"

"I'm sure it does," I said.

"Then couldn't they just row further upriver?" Detective Williams said.

"I guess they could try. But the River is pretty narrow in this section, and the current is strong. It would only take them a couple of paddle strokes to figure it out and then let the River do its thing. You know, just go with the flow."

"Got it."

Rooster headed for the center of the main channel then slowed down. When he was satisfied with the boat's position, he turned the engine off, and we immediately felt the current begin to pull the boat downriver.

"I see what you mean," Detective Williams said.

Rooster turned the searchlight on and began to slowly sweep it back and forth across the waterline.

"There's no way they could have gotten further upriver?" the Chief said.

"Nah," Rooster said without taking his eyes off the water. "I only keep a tiny amount of gas in my rentals. After I had three stolen in a week about five years ago, I learned my lesson. Either they'll be out here in the channel rowing with the current, or they'll be over on our right trying to make it back to shore."

We continued to drift and stare out over the water in silence for several minutes then I caught a glimpse of something off to my right. I nudged Chief Abrams and Rooster and pointed. Rooster swung the searchlight around until it was focused directly on the boat that Jessie was frantically rowing about two hundred yards from shore. When she saw the beam of the searchlight, she began rowing even harder. But after a few strokes, she realized it was futile and placed the oars back in their locks. Chief Abrams took over searchlight duties from Rooster who started the engine and slowly headed toward their boat. Rooster positioned our boat directly upriver from them, then put the boat in neutral and we began drifting straight toward the two women who were huddled close and obviously whispering.

"Show us your hands," Detective Williams said loudly, his hands reaching for his gun. "Hands. Let me see those pretty manicures."

"Really, Detective?" I said, shaking my head. "*Show me your manicures?*"

"Okay, I'm done. That's all I'm going to listen to for one night."

"Don't bet on it," I said, then caught the dirty look the Chief was giving me and let it go.

Both women slowly raised their hands, and I couldn't miss the fear in their eyes.

"Well done. Now, just keep them up in the air where I can see them."

We continued to drift toward them, and Chief Abrams grabbed the bow line without taking his eyes off them. I noticed Titan's fur bristling when he spotted the stolen rental, and his guttural growl echoed across the water. If being out on the water at night in a small boat out of gas with two cops about to descend and arrest you for murder wasn't enough to send a chill up your spine, I was pretty sure Titan's growl would do the trick.

When we were about fifty feet away from the boat, it began to rock, and Jessie appeared to lose her balance, and she reached for the side of the boat to catch herself.

"Hands," Detective Williams said, his gun at his side.

"Hold your horses," Jessie snapped. "I just didn't want to fall in."

What played out over the next several seconds will definitely be retold on a regular basis over the coming years. And I doubt if the story will need much embellishment.

Jessie wobbled back and forth on her legs until she got her balance, then stood straight up, raised her arm and fired at us in one smooth motion.

I heard a loud *whoosh* and saw a flash of light heading straight for our boat I immediately recognized. Detective Williams raised his gun and prepared to fire back, and I jumped toward him.

"No!" I screamed as I shoved him hard. "Don't shoot. It's just a flare gun."

"I can't believe I forgot about the flare gun," Rooster said.

Those were the last words I remember hearing before the flare hit me square in the shoulder then bounced off into the water with a loud hiss. I dropped like a rock onto the deck of the boat, smelled a blend of phosphorous and burning fleece and flesh, and heard the unmistakable sound of someone falling into the water.

Titan starting barking loudly and hopped over the seat and hovered next to me. Rooster grabbed a towel, quickly dipped it in the water, then began swatting at the flames that were beginning to make short work of my coat. My shoulder was initially numb, then an intense burning sensation emerged that my neurons didn't know how to process. Rooster got the flames out, then gently unzipped and helped me out of my jacket. Dazed, I heard Chief Abrams' voice.

"Suzy?" he said, leaning over me. "Are you all right?"

"I think so," I managed to get out. "But I think I'm on fire."

"No, the flames are out," Rooster said, dropping to his knees and resting my head in his lap. He looked up at Chief Abrams who continued to stare down at me in disbelief that I'd been shot. "She'll be fine. You better check on him."

"Okay, will do," Chief Abrams said, then called out. "Are you okay?"

"I said, I'll be fine," I snapped, annoyed at being asked again.

I guess getting shot was enough of an excuse to be a little snarky.

"What?" Chief Abrams said, glancing over his shoulder at me. "I heard you the first time. And I'm very glad you're okay. But I was talking to Detective Williams." He refocused on the water, and I heard the sound of splashing. "Hey, that was a pretty cool move, Detective. Well done."

"Thanks," I heard from off in the distance.

"He drifted right down to their boat," Chief Abrams said glancing back at us and shaking his head in amazement. "Well, I'll be. Wait until you guys see what he's doing."

"We better get him out of the water," I said, grimacing as I sat up and rested on one elbow. "He was already whining about how cold it is."

"I heard that. And I wasn't whining," Detective Williams said from the water. "It was merely an observation." Then he barked a command. "I said, hands up."

Rooster pulled back the burnt section of fabric next to my shoulder and examined the wound.

"Geez, that's a bad burn, Suzy," he said. "We gotta get you to the ER."

"I'm fine," I said, using my good arm to stand. I wobbled a bit, then leaned against the back of the driver seat. "And I have some questions for Missy."

"You're unbelievable," Rooster said, shaking his head.

"Finally, somebody notices."

Chief Abrams tied Rooster's boat to the stolen rental then reached down to help both women onto ours.

"Don't try anything funny," Detective Williams said.

Confused by his comment, I glanced down into the water and realized the detective was holding onto the rental boat with one hand and pointing his gun at Missy and Jessie with the other.

"The water's pretty cold, huh?" I said.

"Yeah, you might say that," he said, his teeth chattering.

"I doubt if your waterlogged gun is even still working," Jessie said as she climbed into the boat.

"You want to try and find out?" the detective said.

Chief Abrams helped Missy into the boat, and she sat down next to Jessie on the padded seat that ran along the transom. He had them both stand back up, did a quick search of both women, then nodded.

"Okay, they're clean," he said, sitting down between them.

"I can't believe I forgot all about the flare gun," Rooster said softly. "I keep them in all my rentals. I'm so sorry, Suzy."

"Don't worry about it, Rooster," I said, slowly making my way to the back of the boat. "You didn't shoot me."

"I'm sorry about that, Suzy," Jessie said, chagrined. "I wasn't aiming at you. I was just trying to set your boat on fire so we could escape."

"Yeah, good plan," I deadpanned, then examined my shoulder that continued to burn and throb. "Man, that really hurts."

I sat down on a bench seat and stared at Missy while the Chief draped a blanket over my shoulders. Missy eventually made eye contact and shrugged. I looked away and focused on Rooster who was wrapping a blanket around the shivering Detective Williams. Then he started the boat and headed back toward the hospital with the rental in tow.

"We'll drop Suzy off first, then you guys can do your thing with those two," Rooster said, glancing over his shoulder. Then he reached into his pocket for his phone.

"That'll work," Chief Abrams said.

I made eye contact with Missy again, and we stared at each other in silence each waiting for the other to go first.

"How did you figure it out?" she said, eventually.

"It wasn't easy," I said. "I almost missed it."

"But then I made some sort of mistake?" she said, frowning.

"No, not really. It was almost perfect. At least it was until you were forced to show up tonight."

"I couldn't run the risk of Bill talking," she said.

"No, you couldn't. And that's what I was counting on."

"He's dead, isn't he?" Missy said.

"Yeah. He never made it out of my mother's garden."

"So, you decided to fake his life."

"See?" I said, glancing at Chief Abrams. "She gets it."

The Chief shot me a dirty look then stared out at the water.

"You need to understand that Jessie had nothing to do with the murders," Missy said.

"Missy, it's okay," Jessie said. "Don't worry about me.

"I know she didn't," I said. "You dragged her into it after you heard Bill was still alive."

"Yes," Missy said, tearing up.

"Getting everyone to believe that you'd be arriving in town the day after Roger got killed was a stroke of genius," I said, focusing on Missy.

"It was," she said, shrugging. "Or so I thought."

"But you were around town the whole time, right?"

"I was. I even went to the trouble of checking into a motel about four hours away, then after I registered, I got back in my car and finished the trip."

"So, where did you stay the night you killed Roger?"

"In my car. In a parking lot a few miles out of town," she said. "But how on earth did you figure out I was the one who killed him?"

"I was in the men's bathroom when you shoved the cyanide capsule down his throat. What was it in?"

"A little gumdrop," Missy said. "He barely even noticed it. Hang on a second. You were in the men's bathroom?"

"Yeah," I said, then realized how strange that sounded. "Long story."

"All the good ones are," she said with a shrug. "You saw us in there?"

"No, I was hiding in the supply closet."

"You really need to get out more," Jessie said.

"Yeah, you don't have to tell me," I said, glancing at her before refocusing on Missy. "And you were whispering the whole time, so I couldn't even hear your voice."

"Then how did you figure it out?" Missy said, frowning again.

"It eventually came to me. At first, we were convinced it had to be one of the women at the rehearsal dinner. And we got it narrowed down to four."

"Charlotte and Trudy. And, of course, Jennifer and Faith," she said.

"Yeah. And after seeing the way Charlotte and Trudy pound the booze, there was no way they could have done it."

"Oh, I'm sure they could have done it," Missy said. "What I think you meant to say was that there was no way they could have gotten away with it."

"A professor to the end, huh?" I said, grinning at her.

"Old habits die hard."

"Yes, they do. And that was something Roger and Bill always managed to prove, right?" I said, glancing back and forth at both women.

"You got that right," Missy said.

"And after I got to know Jennifer and Faith a bit, I was convinced neither one of them was smart enough to pull something like that off," I said.

"The malfunctioning elevators," she said, frowning.

"Exactly," I said. "And after we ruled all four of them out, you two were the only logical suspects left. And since we were convinced that Jessie showing up to work the reception was truly a coincidence, we were left with you."

"It was a coincidence," Jessie said. "I couldn't believe it when I saw Bill and Missy there."

My shoulder pain flared, and I winced. I glanced down at my wound, then regretted it immediately.

"Yuk," I said, frowning. "But the fact that you weren't in town the night Roger got killed was the big stumbling block. Then I remembered a conversation I had with Jackson. I was kidding him about your little late-night stroll in the garden, then he made a comment about how good a kisser you are. And I remembered Roger saying the exact same thing to you in the bathroom."

"That was a mistake," Missy said. "But I'd had a little too much champagne. I never should have done that. The Jackson thing, not Roger. That I don't regret at all."

"You slipped a breath mint into his mouth along with the cyanide capsule, right?"

"I did."

"And since Faith was always gobbling those things by the handful, you thought the cops would suspect her."

"Yes, especially after they found the bag of capsules I slipped into her purse. And the lipstick stain I rubbed on Roger's collar is going to match the one Faith uses."

"Good attention to detail. Still, that was pretty risky, wasn't it?" I said. "You know, transferring a poison pill from your mouth to his?"

"Not really," she said, managing a small laugh. "It was tucked away in the gumdrop and knew it would take a while to dissolve. And Roger was a pig. He was always more than willing to open wide for me."

"At the risk of repeating myself, yuk," I said, frowning. "So, you just showed up at the restaurant and waited for him to go the men's room?"

"Actually, I was expecting him to step outside to have a cigarette," Missy said. "But I was convinced the bathroom was empty when he went in, and I just followed him. Somehow I missed seeing you go in."

"What were you whispering about in there? Did you tell him you wanted to talk about a possible reconciliation?" I said.

"Oh, no way," she said, grimacing and shaking her head. "It was more like how about once more for old-time sake. Obviously, he was all over the prospect of that. After that, I got out the heck out of there and waited to be told the news after I'd arrived in town the next morning."

"Well, I have to say that you were very convincing," I said.

"Not convincing enough. Was it your idea to fake the scene at the hospital tonight?"

"It was," I said, nodding.

"Brilliant."

"Thanks."

"But you weren't sure who the killer was at the time, right? That was just a clever ruse to get me to show my face."

"Yeah, up until today, I was wondering if Faith or Jennifer might actually come strolling into the room. Then that all changed when we were out on the boat."

"I'm not following you," Missy said. "I don't remember anything happening out there."

"Jessie and I were chatting about her childhood, and she mentioned what happened to her parents. She used the foster-child story on me, and at the time I didn't give it a lot of thought. Then it started to bother me. I mean, why would a young girl about to inherit a lot of money end up in foster care? So, I called the Chief and asked him to see what he could find out."

"Your parents' accident was all over the place when I searched for it," the Chief said. "Along with several follow-up articles about your...problems."

"You mean my meltdown," Jessie said.

"You were only six," the Chief said. "I can't imagine what that would be like. After I located the name of the place you were taken, I asked Detective Williams to run it down. He's got more juice than a small-town cop. And he ended up speaking with a Dr. Charles."

"I wouldn't believe a word that quack has to say," Jessie said.

"Even the part about Missy being your assigned sponsor?" I said, glancing back and forth at them.

They both fell silent and looked down at the deck.

"I can't go back there, Missy."

"Hang in there, Jess. We'll figure something out."

"How did you two meet?" I said.

"I did some work at the place where Jessie was staying. I was doing research on the rehabilitation of children trying to recover from serious childhood trauma."

"Was that before or after you escaped and stole the car?"

Jessie flinched, then looked up at me.

"Way before."

"Jessie is fine," Missy said, tearing up. "At least she was until I got her involved in this mess. But those two animals wouldn't leave her alone."

"You're forgetting that sleeping with them was my choice," Jessie said.

"You slept with Roger as well?" I said, surprised.

"Actually, I slept with him before Bill. They were always hanging out in a couple of bars the students went to," Jessie said. "I had no idea he was Missy's ex-husband. And he had no idea she was my sponsor."

"Weird," I said, then looked over at Missy. "And when you found out, you were determined not to let them do the same thing they did to you and Jill's family." I exhaled loudly as my neurons finally relaxed when the last piece of the puzzle snapped into place. "That was your motive, right? You just didn't want to have the same thing happen to Jessie."

"You're good," Missy said, nodding. "It simply had to stop. And Jess wasn't capable of saying no. They were predators, and I was obviously familiar with what both of them were capable of. I was convinced that both of them would end up treating Jess like a piece of trash and send her into a major tailspin."

"I told you I was fine," Jessie snapped. "But you had to stick your nose into my business."

"I was trying to protect you. Because I knew what they were capable of," Missy said, protesting. "They were going to use you then toss you away like a used tissue."

"I was having fun," Jessie said. "For the first time in my life."

"Did Missy talk you into helping her with the cover-up?" I said.

"No, as soon as she told me what she'd done, I raised my hand," Jessie said. "I didn't think it was possible we'd ever get caught. But when I started to think about what might happen to me, I freaked out, changed my mind, and decided to leave town. But Missy stopped me."

"It would have looked suspicious. And we were so close. We would've been on the road by now," Missy said, tears streaming down her face. "If you hadn't ruined it."

"Sure, sure," I said, nodding. "Sorry about that."

I felt the boat slow down and noticed we were approaching the hospital dock where two hospital staff were already waiting. They were bouncing up and down in their scrubs and shivering in the cold night air. Standing next to them were two state policemen. I was sure they were also freezing their butts off, but they were doing a good job of hiding it.

"It is always this cold in late May?" Jessie said, hugging herself.

"Sometimes," I said, wincing and gently rubbing my shoulder.

Chief Abrams got to his feet after Rooster brought the boat to a stop at the dock.

"Okay, let's go," he said to Missy and Jessie.

They gave me a quick wave then headed for the steps along the side of the boat. Then Missy turned around.

"You'll take good care of my babies, right?" she said, tears streaming down her face.

"We will," I said. "That's one thing you won't have to worry about, Missy."

"I guess it's a start," she said, then climbed out of the boat.

I watched the two policemen handcuff both of them, then escort them up the path that led to the hospital. Detective Williams climbed up onto the dock, the blanket still wrapped around him. He was met by one of the hospital staff who walked next to him as they headed up the hill. Rooster and Chief Abrams helped me up onto the dock and continued to watch me closely.

"Are you sure you're okay?" Rooster said.

"I'll be fine," I said, grimacing.

"That's good," Chief Abrams said. "Because if you weren't, we'd be in a world of hurt."

"What?" I said, staring at him.

He nodded at the path where my mother was hustling down toward the dock, trailed closely by Josie.

"Uh-oh," I said, then glanced back and forth at Chief Abrams and Rooster. "Just play it cool and let me do all the talking, okay?"

"No argument from me," Chief Abrams said.

My mother came to a stop directly in front of me, obviously concerned about my well-being. She examined my shoulder without touching it, then gently probed the outside of the wound with her fingers. I flinched and glared at her.

"Hey, go easy with the nails, Mom."

"You got shot," she said, glancing around at all three of us.

"Just with a flare gun," I said, shrugging. "It just grazed me. I'm fine."

"I think we'll let the doctor make that decision," she said, staring at the wound that continued to ooze copious amounts of blood.

"It's just a flesh wound."

"Yes, I can see that. And a whole lot of flesh at that. Rooster, Chief, how did this happen?"

They glanced at each other, then bit their lips, and looked over at me.

"It was my fault, Mom. I was trying to stop Detective Williams from shooting back, and I sort of walked right into the flare when I pushed him overboard." I looked at the Chief and Rooster. "That pretty much sums it up, right?"

"Yeah, that's what I remember," Rooster said.

"Yup," the Chief said, rocking back and forth on his heels.

"Okay," my mother said, refocusing her glare on me. "Let's get you inside so the doctor can take a look at you. But this is far from over, young lady."

"You might want to go easy on me, Mom. I did just solve two murders. No thanks to the Fife twins."

"What?" she said, frowning. "Twins?"

"She's probably just in shock," Chief Abrams blurted.

"Never mind," I said, ignoring the look he was giving me and spotting the remaining staff member heading toward us pushing a wheelchair. "Hey, Johnny. How are you doing?"

"A bit better than you from the look of things, Suzy," he said. "Your chariot awaits."

"Nah, I don't need that," I said, then took a look at the long pathway that led back up to the hospital. Deciding that it probably wasn't the best night to begin my long overdue exercise regimen, I snuck another peek at the gentle incline, then smiled at Johnny. "On second thought, maybe I will take a ride."

He pushed the wheelchair up the incline, and we followed my mother and Chief Abrams up the path. From what I could tell, the Chief was getting quite an earful, but he only nodded in silence as he picked up the pace. But my mother stayed right with him the entire trip like a terrier nipping at his heels.

"Are you sure you're okay?" Josie said, walking next to the wheelchair.

"Yeah, I'll be fine. But it really hurts. And I think I've got a pretty bad burn."

"You were lucky," she said. "It could have been a lot worse."

"Yeah, I know. But don't tell my mother that."

"I think she's probably going to be able to figure that out all by herself, Suzy."

"Trust me, at times like this, silence and denial are your best friends."

Chapter 23

Despite my strong protests, I was admitted to the hospital overnight so the staff could keep a close eye on the second-degree burn I'd suffered. But I must admit that my protests faded as soon as the painkillers they gave me started to kick in. By the time the staff had cleaned and bandaged my wound, I was groggy and could barely manage a few whispered expletives while they helped me out of my clothes and into one of the dreaded hospital gowns. My mother and Josie hovered throughout the process, then sat down near my bed and chatted with the nurse and doctor as I began to drift off.

I woke up in the middle of the night in complete darkness, thoroughly confused about where I was. Then I felt my shoulder throb, and it all came back to me in a flash. I stared up at the ceiling, and since I was simply too tired to fight back, I let my neurons run wild. But they were drug-addled and made no sense whatsoever.

But I did manage to devote some time to Jessie and Missy and her three labs who'd soon be wondering what had happened to their mama. Over time, I was pretty sure that, unlike Jessie, they'd be able to forget about being left on their own at a very young age and be able to move forward and give their full love and affection to someone else. I was less certain that Jessie would ever be able to do the same. Given her history of mental problems, I was pretty sure she'd be institutionalized instead of imprisoned, and I imagined it would take many years before she could convince the people assigned to watch over her that she was well enough to rejoin the rest of us in mainstream society.

But I had no doubts about what was going to happen to Missy. She was going away for a very long time. And I was sure she would spend many sleepless nights thinking about what she'd done, and how poorly she'd performed carrying out her duties as the person responsible for making sure Jessie was secure and able to cope with life on the outside. More than the two murders, I was certain her failure as the young woman's sponsor would be the thing that kept her awake at night then haunted her dreams.

I'd woken up thirsty, and I reached for the water container. I bumped the tray next to the bed, and the noise woke Josie who was still in one of the chairs next to the bed and barely visible in the dim light.

"What's going on?" she said, still half-asleep. "You need to go to the bathroom?"

"No, I think I can hold it until morning," I said. "But I do need a drink of water."

She turned on the small lamp next to the bed and held the water container close as I sipped from the straw.

"Did my mother go home?" I said, glancing over at the empty chair.

"Yeah, right," Josie said, laughing. "Like that's gonna happen. She left about a half-hour ago to take a walk with Chief Abrams."

"That poor man," I said, managing a small smile. "I better get back on my feet before she wears him down to a nub."

"Oh, don't worry. I'm sure she's saving her best stuff for you," she said, sitting down in the chair. "But maybe it's time you starting thinking about getting out of the crime solving business."

"The first guy dropped dead in our restaurant, Josie," I said, pushing myself further up in bed with my good arm. "And we found the second guy in my mother's garden. It's not like I went looking for it."

"I know, but still," she said, already looking for a way to end the conversation.

"And in case you haven't noticed, I'm pretty good at this stuff."

"Yes, you are. But just a few inches higher and a foot to the right that flare would have either killed you or done so much damage to your face you'd wish it would have," she said. "And you have such a nice face."

"Oh, aren't you sweet."

"Don't let it go to your head," she said, again holding the water container close. "I'm just saying that there are times when you need to step back and let the cops do their thing."

"Like getting stuck in a bathroom doorway?"

"Yeah," she said, grinning. "That is pretty funny. I would have liked to have seen that."

"Aren't you forgetting something?" I said.

"What?"

"You haven't made one crack about my gown."

"I'd never make fun of you while you were hurt or in pain."

"Because they'll be plenty of time for that after I make a full recovery, right?"

"Nothing gets past you."

The door slowly opened, and my mother and Chief Abrams stuck their heads inside.

"What are you doing up?" my mother said, approaching the bed.

"I woke up thirsty."

"Consider yourself fortunate to be able to wake up at all," my mother said.

"Geez, Mom. Let it go," I said, returning her stare. "I got shot in the shoulder by a flare gun. Big deal. I'm sure it happens all the time."

"We'll discuss this further after you get back home," she muttered under her breath.

"I can't wait," I said, then focused on Chief Abrams who was standing behind my mother. "How are you doing, Deputy Fife?"

"I'm fine," the Chief said through a forced, tight-lipped smile.

"I was just having a little chat with the Chief, and we've decided that you will no longer be allowed to participate in any of these shenanigans."

"Yeah, I'm sure that was a mutual decision. Save your breath, Mom."

"Now you listen to me, young lady."

"No, Mom, for once you're going to listen to me," I said, fighting through the fog of the painkillers, my voice rising. "I'm going to live my life the way I choose. And if some of my choices lead me into situations you consider stupid or even dangerous, that's tough noogies for you. So, I suggest you just suck it up and find a way to deal with it. And if you don't like hearing it, that's your problem, not mine."

"Whoa," Josie said, staring at me in disbelief, then at my mother. "I'm sensing a firestorm brewing on the horizon. Maybe we should leave, Chief."

"Stay right where you are," I snapped, then immediately softened. "I may need witnesses."

My mother burst out laughing and shook her head as she stared at me.

"Well played, darling. It looks like some of the life lessons I've tried to instill about being tough and not taking crap from anybody are finally starting to take root."

I sat back in bed and gnawed at my bottom lip. Once again, my mother had managed to snatch the upper hand back just before she was about to go down in a crushing defeat.

"How do you do that, Mom?"

"You're good at solving murders," she said with a shrug. "I'm an expert with the snappy comeback."

"Okay, we'll call it a draw," I said, nodding.

"A draw? Nice try, darling. I don't think so."

The door opened, and a nurse entered. She glanced around, frowning.

"It's a little late for visitors, don't you think?" the nurse said. "I just came in to take a quick look at that wound. Are you still in pain?"

"Actually, I am," I said, glancing over at my mother. "But at the moment, it's another part of my body that's hurting."

"Funny, darling."

The nurse ushered everyone out, changed my bandage that was already bloody, then gave me another painkiller.

"Will I be able to go home tomorrow?"

"Yes, I'm pretty sure you will," she said, fluffing my pillows. "But you'll need to take it easy for a few days at least."

"That won't be a problem," I said, yawning. "I'm really good at that."

"Get your rest."

She left the room, then I nodded off again. And I didn't wake up until the smell of coffee and bacon invaded my dreams and gradually pulled me from my sleep. I opened my eyes expecting to see a staff person holding a tray of hospital food but instead saw Chef Claire standing next to my bed holding a large traveler mug of coffee and an object I recognized immediately even though it was wrapped in aluminum foil.

"Good morning," Chef Claire said. "How are you feeling?"

"Okay, I think," I said, sitting up in bed. "But not as good as I will be in a few minutes. Is that what I think it is?"

"It is," she said unwrapping the sandwich and handing it to me.

It was called The Josie and was on our lunch menu at the restaurant, but we made them at home on a regular basis for breakfast. Two over easy eggs and way too much bacon sat between a waffle that was cut in half and slathered with an apple-maple butter. I took a bite and was glad I was sitting in bed because the sandwich was a total knee-buckler and with only one good arm I don't think I would have been able to break my fall.

"Where's Josie?" I mumbled through a mouthful as I reached for a napkin.

"She's still outside," Chef Claire said, laughing. "She couldn't wait five minutes until we got here to eat hers, and she ended up dripping egg all over my car. I told her she couldn't come in until she cleaned up her mess."

"Good for you. Not that she's going to learn her lesson. Have you seen my mother around?"

"She's at the front desk handling your discharge paperwork."

"That's great. I can't wait to get home and see the dogs."

"I can't believe you got shot," Chef Claire said.

"Yeah, me either. I don't recommend it."

"You were very lucky," she said, sitting down. "You need to start being a bit more careful, Suzy. The place just wouldn't be the same without you."

"I'm not going anywhere."

"Josie says we're going to be able to keep the three labs."

"For now," I said. "Until we find a very good home for all three."

"They're already in a very good home. And Dente would never forgive me if we let somebody adopt them," she said, laughing. "I still can't believe Missy did it. And she shoved a cyanide capsule down their throats with her tongue?"

"Yeah, Yuk, huh?"

"I guess that would depend on who the guy was, right? The tongue, not the cyanide thing."

"Yeah, got it. Thanks for clearing that up."

"The French Kiss of Death. That would be a good title for a book."

"A little dark, don't you think?" I said, giving it some thought. "I'd probably try to work a dog reference in. Something like *The Lovable Labs*."

The door opened, and my doctor and a different nurse entered, followed by my mother and Josie.

"Good morning, Suzy," the doctor said, leaning down to examine my wound.

"Hey, Doc. I hear I'm getting out of here."

"Yes, you are. Just as soon as I take another look at this. I already went over the discharge instructions with your mom. Just make sure you do exactly what she tells you for the next week."

"Geez, Doc, that's like giving her a license to steal," I said, frowning. "I thought we were friends."

"Regardless," he said, standing upright and nodding in approval. "Okay, that looks even better than I'd hoped. But if it starts to show the least amount of infection, you come back and see me immediately. Got it?"

"Got it. Thanks, Doc."

"Okay, you're free to go," he said, starting to head for the door. Then he stopped and turned back. "Oh, by the way, feel free to keep the gown."

"What?" I said, frowning at him.

"The gown. Keep it," he said, glancing around. "Your mother said something about how you might want to wear it the next time you're back in Cayman. She said your boyfriend, some guy named Gerald, would love seeing you in it. Personally, I don't get it, but whatever floats your boat, right?" Then he gave my mother a conspiratorial wink and waved over his shoulder as he left the room laughing.

Josie and Chef Claire roared with laughter, and I was forced to wait it out.

"That's the way you're gonna play it, huh, Mom?"

"I'm just having a little fun with you, darling," she said with an evil grin. "Suck it up."

I flinched, then slowly made my way out of bed and headed to the bathroom to get dressed, holding the back of my gown closed with one hand. After I finally managed to get my jeans on, I asked Josie to help me with my sweater, and a few minutes later, I was standing outside the hospital wearing a sling and enjoying the feel of the warm sun on my face. I was about to climb into the passenger seat of my mom's Range Rover when a car pulled into the parking lot next to us. Faith and her mother got out and made their way toward us. Faith and Josie glared at each other the entire time.

"We heard about what happened," Jennifer said. "I'm so glad you're okay."

"Thanks," I said. "Are you guys heading home?"

"Yes, we are," Jennifer said, staring out at the River. "I still can't believe it. Of all the people who would do something like that, Missy would have been way down my list."

"I was very surprised, too," I said.

"You thought one of us did it, didn't you?" Faith said, focusing her glare on me.

"Yeah, for a while, I thought you might have," I said, nodding.

"Sorry to disappoint you," Faith said.

"Faith, please. Not today," Jennifer said.

"Like I'd waste my time killing either one of them," Faith said, then refocused on Josie. "But on the other hand, you're a different story altogether."

"Bring it on, Beelzebub," Josie said softly.

"Ladies, please," my mother said and waited until both of them settled down. "Well, Jennifer, it was a pleasure meeting you, and I'm so sorry things played out the way they did."

"Well, at least it's one wedding I know I'll never forget," she said, shaking her head. "Okay, Faith, let's go. Thanks again for everything. Oh, Trudy and Charlotte asked me to pass along their thanks as well. At least, I think that's what they said. They were pretty hammered last night."

"You're all welcome, anytime," my mother said.

I opened the car door, and Josie placed a hand on my good shoulder to help me up into the car.

"Oh, Josie," Faith said with a lilting voice. "There's just one more thing."

"What's that?" Josie said, turning around.

Faith launched herself forward and threw a roundhouse sucker punch that Josie barely managed to duck. Josie immediately returned fire with a one-two, left hook, right uppercut combination. Both punches landed hard, and Faith dropped like a rock onto the pavement.

"Oh, Faith," her mother said, staring down at her daughter who was dazed and bleeding profusely from the nose. "What on earth is wrong with you?"

"I think it's that pesky elevator thing," I said, staring down at the ground. "She's going to need to get checked out." I nodded in the direction of the hospital.

Jennifer helped her daughter to her feet and glared at her.

"Now you've put us way behind schedule," she said, dragging her by the collar toward the front door. "I hope you're happy with yourself."

We watched them go then looked around at each other.

"Don't you think you should have warned her you'd taken self-defense classes?" I said.

"It wouldn't have made any difference. She's too dumb to listen to reason," Josie said, shaking both her hands then starting to rub them. "Man, I gotta stop doing that."

"Well, I would certainly hope so, dear," my mother said. "It's not exactly what I would call ladylike behavior."

"No, it's not that," Josie said, wincing as she glanced down at her hands. "I need these things to operate with."

Epilogue

Early the next morning we drove Sammy and Jill to the small airport on the edge of town where a private jet was waiting to take them to Grand Cayman. Josie and Chef Claire helped them with their bags, while my duties, due to the sling I was wearing, were relegated to a quasi-supervisory role. After we'd said our goodbyes and wished them the best for a wonderful honeymoon, we waited until they boarded, then waved as the plane rolled down the airstrip.

I climbed in the backseat of Chef Claire's car, and Josie turned around and held out a bag of bite-sized. I grabbed a small handful with my good hand.

"You going to need any help opening those?" Josie said.

"Yeah, right," I said, using my teeth to rip open the first chocolate morsel.

Chef Claire drove back to the house, dropped us off in front of the Inn, then headed for the restaurant. We went inside and found Josie's first appointment already waiting. I touched base with the rest of the staff, reviewed the day's calendar, then stood leaning against the registration counter looking around for something to do. Michelle, one of our newer techs, sat down behind the counter and frowned at me.

"Aren't you supposed to be resting?" she said.

"Yes, she is," Josie said, pausing on her way into an exam room. "You're not supposed to be here."

"No, I'm okay," I said.

"Suzy," Josie said firmly. "You're supposed to stay off your feet for a few days. Why don't you head up to the house and spend the day playing with the dogs?"

"Really, I'm fine."

"Don't make me call your mother."

"You wouldn't dare."

"Watch me," Josie said, reaching for her phone.

"All right," I said, shaking my head. "I'm leaving. But how about I make lunch and bring it down later?"

"That you can do," Josie said, giving me a finger wave as she headed for the exam room.

I spent the next few days doing as she suggested, and being surrounded by seven dogs while I convalesced was better than any of the painkillers I'd been prescribed.

After a week, the sling came off, and I was able to use my arm for most daily activities. But my shoulder still ached, and it looked like I was definitely going to be left with a scar, a not so friendly reminder of my encounter with a flare gun that had been fired by a scared, young woman who'd gotten caught up in the moment and decided she was out of options. Josie and Chef Claire are both encouraging me to get a tattoo to hide the scar. I'm thinking about it, but I'm leaning toward keeping it as is to serve as a reminder of how easy it is for your life to be over in a flash if you stop paying attention.

Either that or a puppy tattoo.

I did call Jessie after I heard she'd been institutionalized again, and we spoke at length. She seemed relatively stable but was still furious about being held against her will and unable to resume her life as a college student. I felt bad for her and felt even worse when I realized that there was really nothing I could do for her. She has a very long road to recovery ahead of her, and she's going to have to do pretty much all the driving.

I tried twice but was unable to connect with Missy. Either the prison where she was being held wasn't letting her take calls, or she simply didn't want to speak with me. But through Detective Williams, I was able to follow the progress of her case that was heading for a speedy trial and a very lengthy sentence. The detective and I made our peace after he apologized for his behavior, and I promised not to get snarky with him or bring up the fact that he somehow managed to get wedged in a doorway at the exact moment my life was in danger.

Really? A doorway?

Unfreakingbelievable.

I've gone back and forth more times than I care to admit about what really motivated Missy to kill the two men. And every time I find myself dwelling on that question, I always end up stuck in a loop with a neuron headache. The closest I can come to a conclusion is that it might actually have had a lot more to do with Missy's history with both men than it did about her trying to protect Jessie from herself. And I wondered if Jessie's situation was simply a good excuse for committing the murders and then rationalizing them away. But given Missy's intelligence and educational background, she has a much better chance of decoding her real motive than I do, and she's certainly going to have a lot of time to figure it out. And when she does, maybe she'll be kind enough to explain it to me someday.

Sammy and Jill returned from their honeymoon content and tanned and still basking in their newly-married glow. The fact that her beloved godmother had killed two men continues to torment her, and the death of her father lingers just below the surface. Occasionally, I'll find her sobbing by herself in various sections of the Inn, but instead of burying it, she's definitely dealing with her grief, and it appears that in some strange way it's making her stronger and bringing her and Sammy even closer together. I like their chances going forward.

Chief Abrams, with my mother's help, continued to labor under a self-imposed sense of guilt about how close I'd come to getting killed and decided to try and make it up to me by hovering. At first, I thought his constant dropping by to see if I needed anything during my initial recovery was thoughtful and cute. Then it started to annoy me. And after a week, I finally had to sit him down for a serious chat about my need for space, how I really wasn't in that much danger that night, and, despite his comical attempt to get through the bathroom door, it wasn't his fault. There was no way Missy was going to be able to get anything in my mouth, and getting hit by the flare was a one in a million combination of a lucky shot and stroke of bad luck. Eventually, he settled down, and our friendship was back on solid ground.

At the moment, he's standing next to me in the kitchen and looking over my shoulder watching me add the final ingredients to the beef stew I'm making. It's Monday, family dinner night, and the adults have the house to themselves now that we've put all seven dogs outside to enjoy the warm evening air and the impending sunset that promises a lot of purple and orange, one of my favorites. The three labs are growing like weeds, and even I'm forced to admit that having seven bruisers in the house can be a bit much. But then I start rolling around the floor with all of them, and I'm toast.

In the living room, I can hear my mother regaling Josie and Chef Claire with a story about one of her recent dates and soon they are all laughing loudly.

"Who's the guy your mom is talking about?" the Chief said, grabbing a wooden spoon and stirring the stew.

"I don't know," I said, chopping Italian parsley. "But based on what's she saying, he's obviously not a keeper."

"What about you?"

"What about me?" I said, pausing from my chopping to look up at him.

"Are you any closer to finder a keeper?"

"I haven't found anybody, much less know if he might be a keeper," I said as I grabbed a handful of parsley and dropped it into the stew.

"Maybe you just need to start looking a little bit harder," he said, slowly stirring.

"Maybe you need to stop spending so much time around my mother," I said, cocking my head at him. "What's going on, Chief? Has giving me relationship advice been added to your penance?"

"Maybe."

"Unbelievable," I said, shaking my head.

"But if she asks, make sure you tell her I made an effort."

"I'll do that, Chief," I said, laughing as I headed for the fridge. I rummaged around but couldn't find what I was looking for. "I can't believe it."

"What?"

"I forgot to get sour cream," I said, closing the fridge and wiping my hands on a dish towel. "I need to run to the store. I'll be right back."

"No, I'll go," he said, reaching into his pocket for his car keys.

"Are you sure?"

"Not a problem," he said, heading for the door.

"Thanks. I appreciate it."

"I'll be right back."

"Hey, Chief."

"Yeah?"

"You need any help getting out the door?"

"Don't get smart with me, *young lady*."

I laughed hard.

"Oh, that was so close. You almost had it."

Made in the USA
Las Vegas, NV
03 June 2021

24137169R00142